The Royal Ballet School Diaries

Kate's special secret

"I just cannot wait to meet Lim Soo May!" Naomi cried, clasping her hands together. She pretended to address the figures in the poster, wagging her finger at them. "Now, you must choose *me* for your masterclass, do you hear? Me – Naomi Crawford! Remember that name, please!"

Lara and Ellie got into the spirit of things and started begging the picture of Lim Soo May to choose them as well. And then Ellie noticed that Kate wasn't joining in. In fact she was looking distinctly uncomfortable.

Look out for more stories from
The Royal Ballet School:

08958

The Royal Ballet School Diaries

Kate's special secret

Alexandra Moss

SCHOLASTIC

For Holly Powell,
with lots of love

Special thanks to Sue Mongredien

Scholastic Children's Books,
Euston House, 24 Eversholt Street,
London, NW1 1DB, UK
a division of Scholastic Ltd
London ~ New York ~ Toronto ~ Sydney ~ Auckland
Mexico City ~ New Delhi ~ Hong Kong

Published in the UK by Scholastic Ltd, 2006
Series created by Working Partners Ltd

Copyright © Working Partners Ltd, 2005

10 digit ISBN 0 439 95975 6
13 digit ISBN 978 0439 95975 9

Printed by Nørhaven Paperback A/S, Denmark

10 9 8 7 6 5 4 3 2 1

Prologue

Dear Diary,

I'm all ready to go back to The Royal Ballet School tomorrow for the start of the summer term! I can't believe Easter vacation is over already – it's flown by. I've had such a fun time hanging out in Oxford with my old friends Phoebe and Bethany. Bethany has been preparing for her Grade Three ballet exams and wanted me to practise with her a couple of afternoons. I'd forgotten how good a dancer she is – it's such a shame she didn't make it to The Royal Ballet School with me.

She really begged me to show her some of the steps we've learned en pointe, but I kept hearing Ms Wells saying in her strictest voice how we must never ever EVER practise dancing en pointe without a teacher supervising, so I didn't dare. I did put my pointe shoes on, though — to show Phoebe what they looked like — and I stood en pointe just for a moment. But I didn't do any steps in them — I took them right off again. It would be just my luck to break the rules and promptly injure myself for months on end!

Anyway, here I am, bags packed and injury-free, ready to start the new term tomorrow. I can't wait to go back and see Grace, Lara, Naomi and all my other friends again; I really miss them when we're not together. This time tomorrow I'll be unpacked and ready for the start of summer term — and I'm sure it's going to be an amazing one!

Chapter One

"Heeeere's Ellie Brown!" announced Naomi, as Ellie burst into the long, curving dormitory shared by all twelve of the Year 7 girls at The Royal Ballet Lower School.

Ellie beamed back at Naomi and their other friends who had also recently arrived back – Grace, Lara, Belle, Kate and Bryony. She'd said a quick hello to them when she and her mum had dropped off her bags in the dorm a few minutes earlier, but Ellie knew that none of her friends would tell her anything *really* newsworthy while she still had a parent in tow! After she'd waved her mum off she'd all but sprinted back up the steps to the dorm, in such a hurry was she to catch up with everybody's news.

"Hi, guys!" Ellie called. "Oh, it's sooo great to see you all again."

Ellie felt a particular poignancy as she hugged Naomi. This was going to be Naomi's last term at The Royal Ballet School as, sadly, she'd failed her annual appraisal and had been "assessed out". She now had a place lined up at a performing arts school in Manchester for the coming September, which sounded great, but Ellie felt a pang of sadness every time she thought about Naomi not being at school with the rest of the gang. *Still – all the more reason to make this the best term ever,* she thought quickly.

"So how are you, Ell?" Naomi asked, with one of her usual wide smiles.

Lara elbowed her cheekily before Ellie could reply. "I thought *Madame Naomi* would already know that," she said, referring to Naomi's love of astrology and predicting her friends' futures. "Does your crystal ball need a wee polish?"

Naomi rolled her eyes. "My powers of prediction are a mysterious gift, Lara," she said loftily. "I can't just tune in at will, you know!"

Ellie sputtered with laughter. As usual, Naomi had an answer for everyone and everything. "Going back to your question, I'm great, thanks," she said. "How are you? You're looking very brown – were you away somewhere?"

"Or is it a fake tan?" Kate joked, peering closely at Naomi's complexion.

Naomi looked appalled at the thought. "Fake? How dare you?" she said, pretending to be huffy. "This is pure Manchester sunshine, this is. Didn't you know that I live in the northern Riviera?"

The other girls laughed at such an exaggeration – even Ellie, an American, knew by now that the city of Manchester was better known for its rain than its sunshine.

Half-French Belle, however, who had only been living in England for a few months, looked a little unsure. "I have not heard of this northern Riviera," she said, her dark eyes narrowing suspiciously. "Naomi, are you pulling my arm?"

"I think you mean 'leg'," Grace giggled. "And yes, Belle, she is pulling your leg. Only Naomi calls Manchester the northern Riviera – nobody else!"

"Good afternoon, girls!" came a cheery voice behind them.

Ellie spun around at the sound of Mrs Hall, their housemistress, appearing in the dorm with her usual friendly smile.

"Hello, Mrs Hall!" the girls chorused back to her.

"Welcome back. I hope you've all had a good break over Easter," Mrs Hall said. "I've just got a couple of things to tell you about. There's a list up in the Slip with details of this term's weekend outings. There's going to be a boat trip along the Thames, visits to Hampton Court and Kew Gardens, picnics organized in Richmond Park, and so on. And there are also some evening trips booked to a couple of West End musicals that might interest you. You can sign up for as many as you want, but we need to know numbers as soon as possible. So don't delay in putting your names down – it's first come, first served."

Ellie grinned excitedly at her circle of friends as they listened. She liked the sound of everything!

"I can't wait to see the list of musicals," Naomi declared, her eyes shining. "I'm going to put my name down for all of them!"

Lara winked at her. "This time next year, Naomi, you might even be starring in one of them!" she said.

Ellie squeezed one of Naomi's hands. "Here's hoping," she added. They all knew that flamboyant, extroverted Naomi's dream was to be a West End star.

"Finally, Mr Cartwright, the caretaker, has set up a badminton net in the back garden for anybody to use," Mrs Hall said.

"Cool!" Kate said at once. "I love badminton!"

Ellie had *heard* of badminton, but she'd never played it, and had no idea of the rules. "What do we need to play badminton?" she asked Mrs Hall curiously. "Is it like tennis?"

Mrs Hall smiled at her. "A little," she said. "The rackets are a lot lighter, and you have to hit something called a shuttlecock, rather than a tennis ball." She turned to address the room. "Anyway, Mr Cartwright has a full set of rackets and shuttlecocks that you can borrow," she went on. "And you'll have to book slots of time at the net in advance, OK?"

"Great," Naomi said. "Count me in for some of that."

"As usual, if there's anything that anybody wants to talk to me about, do come and find me later on," Mrs Hall finished. "And enjoy the new term!"

Ellie bounced happily on her bed as their housemistress left the dorm again. "This term is going to be awesome." She sighed contentedly. "I just know it!"

After a leisurely lunch, punctuated by cheers and waves as three more Year 7 girls – Holly, Megan and Scarlett – arrived, Ellie and her friends sat outside with crisp green apples to munch, and caught up on the rest of one another's news. The air was fragrant with the smell of freshly cut grass and, from where they were sitting, they could see that all the trees in neighbouring Richmond Park were sprouting their spring foliage. It seemed like the first time since Ellie had started The Royal Ballet School that it was warm enough to sit outside without having to bundle up in warm jackets.

"This is the life," Lara said, stretching out her bare legs happily. "It was blowing a gale in Ireland when I flew out this morning. And this practically feels like summer – I'll be off to change into my bikini if it gets any warmer!"

Kate looked over at Naomi who was suntanning on her back. "Don't you start – Naomi will be calling this the *southern* Riviera any minute!" she joked.

Belle laughed. "You English, you get so excited about the sun coming out," she said, wrinkling her nose. "In France, we prefer to stay in the shade." She patted her face. "I will be getting my sun hat and sunblock, not a bikini, if it gets any hotter!"

Bryony chewed thoughtfully on a piece of grass. "So, what did everyone get up to over the holidays?" she asked.

Lara twirled a daisy stalk around her finger, her green eyes far away for a moment. "The best thing I did was go body boarding at the beach one day with my cousin and his friends. It was just fabulous." She sighed. "There's nothing like it, riding the waves – and clinging on for dear life!"

Belle shuddered. "Not my cup of tea at all – as the English would say."

"Well, I loved it!" Lara said. "But I've still got the bruises to show for it, unfortunately," she added, rubbing her leg gingerly. "I think I swallowed half the Irish Sea, too!"

"Sounds amazing," said Grace. "The riding the waves bit, I mean. Not the pain and suffering you went through afterwards." Shielding her eyes from the sun's glare, she gazed dreamily up at the clouds scudding across the sky. "Sounds really romantic, too. The sort of thing you see in a film, isn't it?"

Lara snorted. "Romantic? You haven't seen

my cousin and his friends. Spotty teenagers only interested in sports talk, that's what they are." She winked at the others. "Still, if that's your type, Grace, let me know and I'll start matchmaking."

Grace sat up, making a face before she realized that Lara was only joking. "Thanks for the offer – but I'll give it a miss," she chuckled. She turned to Kate. "How about you?"

Kate looked horrified. "I'm not interested in Lara's cousin either!" she exclaimed at once.

Ellie giggled. "I think Grace meant: how was your *vacation*, Kate?"

"Oh!" Kate replied, blushing. "Oh, um . . . well, it was good, thanks. I went away with my mum and stepdad."

"Anywhere nice?" Ellie asked.

Kate shut her eyes and leaned back on the grass. "Saint Petersburg," she replied.

"Russia – wow!" Ellie gasped. "Did you get to see any ballet while you were there?"

"Yes, at the Mariinsky Theatre," Kate replied. "But we saw all sorts of other stuff too," she added.

"Lovely. . ." Bryony said appreciatively. "Lucky you, Kate. The local high street was as far as I got last week!"

Kate's cheeks turned a shade pinker, but before she could say anything else, Naomi was leaning up on one elbow with an inquiring look on her face.

"So what kind of boys *do* you like, Kate?" she asked, before reaching over to nudge her. "Just so we all know for the future."

Kate's eyes popped open at the question, and she looked rather flustered, Ellie thought. "Well, I don't know. . ." she began uncertainly. Then, seeing Naomi's wicked grin, she tossed her glossy black hair and stuck her tongue out at her. "Well, for starters, I wouldn't be interested in a boy if he was as nosy as *you*, Naomi Crawford!"

"Is there another person in the world who *could* be as nosy as me?" Naomi wondered aloud. "Probably not. . ."

"Anyone fancy a game?" came a voice just then. It was Matt, one of the Year 7 boys, clutching four badminton rackets.

Ellie smiled up at him. She and Matt had been friends for a long time.

"Talking of romantic heroes. . ." Lara giggled.

"What's that?" Matt asked, frowning in confusion.

"Nothing, nothing," Naomi replied, with a teasing wink at Kate. "I think Kate had finished telling us . . . *something*, hadn't you, Kate?"

Kate pulled up a handful of grass and threw it at Naomi. "I don't believe I said *anything*, you gossip-monger," she laughed.

Matt's frown deepened as he glanced from Naomi to Kate. "Er. . . If I'm interrupting something private. . ." he began awkwardly.

"You're not," Kate told him. "You are *so* not, Matt!"

"OK. . ." Matt replied, glancing over at Ellie for help.

"Oh, just ignore them," Ellie told him cheerfully. "I'll give it a try," she went on, looking curiously at the long metal rackets in his hand. The racket head was smaller and closer-strung than a normal tennis racket. She stared in interest as Matt pulled out a small white object that seemed to have a rounded end and what she could only describe as a plastic frill on the other end. "Is that the . . . um. . ." She struggled to think of the word. "The cockle?"

There was a roar of laughter, and Naomi clapped her on the back. "A *shuttlecock*, Ellie!" she hooted. "A cockle — I love that!"

Ellie laughed good-humouredly. "Whatever," she said, holding up her hands. "I've never played badminton."

"You don't say," Matt chuckled, tossing the shuttlecock over to Ellie so that she could have a closer look. "What you do is try and catch the cockle on your ear and then do a backflip. . ."

Ellie gave him a push and giggled. "Hey! Quit teasing the ignoramus," she said. "So who's going to play?"

"Me," Grace said, jumping up at once. "My neighbours at home have got a set. I love badminton!"

"Me too," Kate said, getting up quickly and brushing grass off her jeans. She looked grateful at the change of subject, Ellie noticed. Strange – it wasn't like Kate to let Naomi rattle her about anything!

In the end, all of them decided that they wanted to play – as did a couple of

Matt's friends, who turned up a few minutes later. Matt only had the net for an hour, so they decided to take turns to play mixed doubles against one another. Matt tossed a coin to decide the first pairs, and it was Grace and Justin against Kate and Nick.

Just as they were about to start, a mobile trilled.

"That's mine," Kate said. She ran over to find her phone from where she'd left it on the grass. "Hello? Oh . . . hi," she said. She turned to the group. "Sorry, could someone take my place, please?" she asked. And then she sat down some distance away to have her conversation.

Naomi took Kate's place, and Ellie sat back with Lara and Belle to watch the first game begin. She couldn't help a sigh of contentment. It was so, so good to be back!

* * *

Dear Diary,

Today was great! All the excitement of coming back to school and catching up on everybody's news. And we had a really fun afternoon — I learned a new game: badminton! It was really fast and furious, trying to keep the shuttlecock — or cockle, as it is now known! — in the air. We had a mixed-doubles mini-tournament. I was on a team with Matt and we beat Kate and Nick hands-down, only losing in the final to Grace and Justin.

It sounds like there are so many exciting things to look forward to this term, too. It's going to be a corker, as Naomi would say. I know it already!

When the term began officially the next day, it felt wonderful to be back in the ballet studio again with Ms Wells. Ellie could really feel her muscles aching after two hours of hard work, though. "It just goes to show," she said to her friends as they changed out of their regulation pink leotards into their blouses and skirts in the dorm afterwards, "all it takes is a few weeks off and our bodies go to pot."

"Speak for yourself," Naomi said primly, kicking her ballet shoes up into the air and catching them neatly, one by one. "Some of us have been practising hard every day."

Ellie and her friends guffawed. Naomi had never been the hardest worker in ballet class, to say the least – and none of them believed for a minute that she'd really been slaving away at the barre, like she claimed!

"Practising what, exactly?" Kate joked. "Your *acting*?"

"Some call it acting, some call it downright lying," Lara teased, winking at her friend.

Naomi laughed along with them and held her hands up. "OK, OK, I admit it," she said. "All I practised was lying in the sun with the odd bit of shopping and horoscope-reading thrown in for good measure. But don't tell Ms Wells that, anybody!"

By Tuesday afternoon, Ellie was starting to feel as if she'd never been away from The Royal Ballet School. She and the other students were always so busy there, going from one class to the next, that she hardly had time to think about home.

The last class of the day on Tuesday was swimming, which Ellie loved. Ms Turner, their PE teacher, had them warming up. "Ten lengths each of you, starting . . . NOW!" she called.

There was a loud splash as all of the girls launched themselves away from the edge of the pool. Ellie kicked herself energetically away from the side and swam the first few metres underwater, relishing the cool blue silence of it. She was a good swimmer, strong and fast, and enjoyed the feeling of being supported by the water.

As she was near the end of the pool on her second length, Ellie looked up to see that Ms Allison, the school secretary, had come into the pool room and was speaking with Ms Turner.

Ellie watched as Ms Turner listened, nodded, and then turned her glance to search the pool for someone. Ellie wondered who she was looking for. Ms Turner then went over to the end of the pool where one of the girls was just finishing a length and squatted down to speak with her. Ellie squinted to see – it was Kate.

By the time Ellie reached the end of the pool herself, Ms Turner had finished speaking with Kate and was walking away again. Ellie flipped over to change direction – and then paused before setting off again, her curiosity getting the better of her. "What did Ms Turner want?" she asked Kate.

Kate was looking puzzled. "She wants me to

go and see Miss Purvis after this class," she replied, shrugging. "But she didn't say why."

Ellie's eyes widened. Miss Purvis was the head of the Lower School. "Weird," she commented. "I wonder what's going on?"

By now, Lara and Naomi had swum over, too, and had caught Kate's words.

"Miss Purvis wants to see you?" Lara repeated, her eyebrows raising until they'd almost disappeared under her swimming cap. "Ooh, Kate – what have you been up to?"

Naomi wagged a finger at her. "Been a naughty girl, have we?" she joked.

Kate's face was blank. "I can't think of anything terrible I've done," she said. She sank her shoulders under the water while she thought. "The only thing I—"

But before Kate could finish her sentence, Ms Turner was striding over towards them, her trainers squeaking on the wet tiles. "Don't tell me you've finished warming up already, have you, girls?" she asked, raising her eyebrows. "No? Then get on with it, please. This is a swimming lesson, not a pool party!"

It was only after class, when Kate had gone to see Miss Purvis, that Ellie and the others started their speculations once again.

"Surely she's not really in any trouble," Belle mused aloud, squeezing the water out of her swimsuit. "I've never known Kate to put a foot wrong at school."

Ellie nodded in agreement, and couldn't help smiling at the Parisian girl's love of using her newly learned English expressions.

"Ah – that's because she's a ballerina, Belle," Naomi said. "Put a *foot* wrong – get it?"

Ellie rolled her eyes at Naomi's terrible joke. "Yes we got it! Belle's right, though," she added. "Kate's not exactly a troublemaker, is she? Not like you, Naomi."

"Ouch!" Naomi squealed, pretending to be

hurt. "Less of that, please, Ellie Brown! I think we all know that I'm a model of good behaviour in this school!"

A giggle went around. "Ri-i-i-ight," Ellie said in a disbelieving drawl. "Ooh – was that a pig flying through the changing room I just saw?"

"It's bound to be something boring that Miss Purvis wants to talk to Kate about," Lara said, rolling up her towel neatly.

"Yes, probably some dull administration stuff," Grace suggested. "Form-filling, parents' signatures, that kind of thing."

"Yeah, you're probably right. Let's go and get ready for dinner anyway," Ellie said, gathering up her swimsuit and towel. "She can tell us all about it in the canteen."

Ellie and the others sat at their usual table in the canteen when Kate walked in. Ellie watched her take a tray and choose her food.

The slightly guarded expression on Kate's pretty face gave no indication as to what had gone on in Miss Purvis's office.

"Everything all right?" Naomi asked as Kate joined them.

"Yes, fine," Kate replied. She seemed to be concentrating hard on unwrapping her juice straw, and didn't look anybody in the eye.

"So, what did she want?" Lara asked bluntly. "Miss Purvis, I mean."

Kate waved a hand airily. "Oh, nothing really," she said, pushing her straw into the carton and taking a drink. She still wasn't meeting anybody in the eye, Ellie noticed. "Just boring stuff, you know. Too dull to talk about."

There was a slightly awkward silence. Ellie stared hard at Kate. Too dull to talk about? Somehow she wasn't convinced by Kate's words.

"Kate, are you *sure* that everything is all

right?" Belle asked eventually, putting a kind hand on Kate's arm. "You can tell us anything, you know."

"Yes, honestly, everything is fine," Kate said breezily. "This lasagne looks good. I'm starving!"

OK, Ellie thought to herself. So Kate wasn't going to tell them anything else. Strange!

After a slight pause, the conversation switched to what was on television that evening as Naomi reminded them all that their favourite soap opera was on later.

"Did you *see* it last week?" She sighed dramatically. "I thought Jake was going to *kill* Max, didn't you? He was so furious!"

"I know!" Grace exclaimed. "I can't wait to see what happens tonight."

"We'll have to save seats in the common room, I think," Ellie joked. "*Everyone* is going to be in there watching it."

"So right," Naomi said, fiddling with her watch. "There – I've even set my alarm so we don't miss it!"

After dinner, Ellie and the others went up to the common room. They had some maths homework to do and Ellie was finding it a little bit tough. She was relieved when Naomi's watch started bleeping.

"Quick, everyone!" Naomi called out.

A couple of the Year 8 girls were already camped out on one side of the huge L-shaped sofa. Naomi immediately hurled herself on to the other side and spread her arms protectively across the rest of it. "Ellie, Lara, come on, girls. Chop, chop," she ordered. "We can get five of us on here, easy."

Ellie, Lara, Grace and Belle squeezed on to the sofa with Naomi, and Bryony pulled up a beanbag. Holly and Megan grabbed big cushions to sit on as the room slowly filled up.

Jessica, Ellie's Year 8 guide, came in and perched on the arm of a sofa, as did Carli, her best friend. Before long, practically every girl from Year 7 and 8 was in there, chattering excitedly.

The only person who wasn't there, Ellie suddenly realized, was Kate. Had she forgotten the show was on?

"Back in a minute," she whispered to Grace as the opening credits played on the screen.

Ellie ran into the dorm and found Kate writing in her diary. "Hey, Kate – aren't you coming to watch TV with us?"

Kate shook her head. "I'm going to have an early night, I think," she said, stuffing her diary hurriedly in her drawer. Then she turned to get out her pyjamas, so that her back was to Ellie.

Ellie hesitated. "Oh. OK then," she said, frowning a little in surprise. Normally Kate never missed an episode – in fact, normally,

Kate would have bagged herself a good seat half an hour ago! Ellie hovered uncertainly for a moment. "Is everything all right?" she asked. "Only. . . You've been kind of quiet since you went to see Miss Purvis."

Kate still didn't turn to look at Ellie. "I'm fine," she said, shaking out her pyjamas.

There was something odd about her tone. Something Ellie couldn't put a finger on. "Well," Ellie replied uncertainly. "It's just that it's not like you to—"

Before she could finish her sentence, though, Kate had interrupted. "Oh, go on, then," she said, bundling her pyjamas back under her pillow. "On second thoughts, I *will* come and watch TV. Thanks, Ellie."

"You're welcome," Ellie said, as Kate strode past her out of the dorm.

Weird, Ellie thought, a little taken aback at Kate's abrupt about-face. Was she missing something? It seemed almost as if Kate had changed her mind about watching TV with everyone in order to end their conversation.

But that's crazy, Ellie told herself as she pushed open the door of the common room and squeezed back into her space next to Grace. *I was only asking Kate if she was all right — it wasn't like I'd asked anything very personal.*

The programme started and Ellie became glued to the screen, holding her breath to see what was going to happen next.

Ten minutes into the show, however, Ellie happened to glance across at Kate. Her friend wasn't even watching the television. She was staring down at the pattern on the beanbag she was sharing with Bryony, deep in thought.

Ellie frowned as she gazed at her friend's distracted expression. There was definitely *something* going on that Kate wasn't telling them about.

❋ ❋ ❋

Dear Diary,

Kate's acting very strangely. She was called in to see Miss Purvis earlier today, and since then she hasn't been herself at all. She's usually so lively, and wants to join in with everything – yet this evening it was as if her mind was somewhere else. When I asked if she was all right, she said nothing was wrong. I hope that's true. Surely she would confide in us if something was seriously wrong. Wouldn't she?

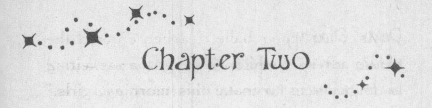

Chapter Two

The following morning, Ellie and the other Year 7 girls made their way to their daily ballet class as usual. Ellie absolutely loved having two whole hours of ballet before her academic classes began. She just couldn't imagine going to a normal school now. How did other people manage without dancing every day? She really didn't understand how they could stand it!

Ellie and her friends peeled off their sweatsuits and tucked their feet into their ballet shoes before they began limbering up as usual. Ellie began stretching out her neck and shoulders, making sure each muscle felt warm and relaxed.

Ms Wells, their ballet teacher, entered the studio after a while. "I've got an exciting announcement to make this morning, girls," she said, her eyes shining.

Immediately, everybody stopped what they were doing and turned to listen. Ellie's heart skipped a beat. What was their teacher about to tell them? Something big, no doubt. Ms Wells's previous announcements had included telling them they would be auditioning for parts in The Royal Ballet's Christmas production at the Royal Opera House – and also telling them about the crucial Year 7 performance appraisals, which had then taken place last term.

"Everybody listening?" Ms Wells asked, looking around at the girls' expectant faces. "OK. The news is that a documentary is going to be made about two famous graduates of The Royal Ballet School: Lim Soo May and Christopher Blackwell. I'm sure you've all heard of them."

Ellie nodded, as did everybody else in the studio. What aspiring ballerina *hadn't* heard of Lim Soo May and Christopher Blackwell? They had gone on to become world-famous dancers and had fallen in love. Together, they had danced the principal roles in almost every famous ballet around the world to great international acclaim and sold-out theatres. *But what does the documentary being made about them have to do with the Lower School?* Ellie wondered.

Smiling, Ms Wells gestured around the studio. "Soo May and Christopher would both have had classes here, just like you, when they were Royal Ballet School students themselves. And the documentary is going to feature them returning to both the Lower School and the Upper School to meet the students of today."

An excited buzz went around the room. *Wow!* Ellie thought. Lim Soo May and

Christopher Blackwell visiting their school! *How awesome is that?*

"That's not all. . ." Ms Wells went on, her eyes sparkling. "While filming Soo May and Christopher's visit here, the documentary makers want to show them giving special coaching to six selected Year 7 students."

Ellie gulped. Six selected *Year 7* students? Had Ms Wells *really* just said that? The studio had fallen into awed silence. You could have heard a hairpin drop, it was so quiet. Ellie felt as if she could hardly breathe with excitement as she waited to hear what their teacher would tell them next.

"Soo May and Christopher will come along with Ms Bell to sit in on a Year 7 girls' and a Year 7 boys' ballet class – from which three girls and three boys will be chosen for special coaching," Ms Wells went on. "Soo May will then give a masterclass to three of you girls, and Christopher will do the same with three

Year 7 boys." She grinned at the row of wide eyes and amazed expressions in front of her. "So . . . what do you think of that?"

"WOW!" Naomi cried at once. "That is sooo fab!"

"Lim Soo May. . . She is just *formidable*!" Belle exclaimed, slipping into French in her excitement. "I can't wait to tell my friends in Paris. They will be so envious, I think!"

Lara was jumping up and down, her green eyes shining. "I can't *believe* they're going to be here, watching us! US!"

"Neither can I!" Ellie squealed, squeezing hands with Grace. She couldn't stop smiling. Lim Soo May and Christopher Blackwell – it was like some kind of wonderful dream. "This is happening, isn't it?" she asked a beaming Bryony. "I'm not asleep and dreaming it all, am I?" She held out her arm. "Pinch me, just to see!" Bryony enthusiastically did as Ellie asked. "Ow! OK, now I know that I'm not dreaming. . ." Ellie said with a grin, as she rubbed her arm.

Grace put her hand up. "Ms Wells, why do you keep calling her 'Soo May'?" she asked. "I thought May was her surname."

Ms Wells shook her head, but before she could explain further, Kate began to speak.

Because Kate was half-Korean herself, she knew the answer. "Lim Soo May is Korean, and in most Asian cultures the surname – the family name – is put first," Kate told Grace. She noticed that everyone was listening to her and turned red. "Something like that, anyway," she muttered, looking down at the floor.

"So Lim is Soo May's family name," Grace said.

"That's right," Ms Wells said. Then she glanced up at the wall clock. "Goodness, we'd better get today's class started. I'll give you further information on the documentary as soon as I have it. Right now, though, I want you to put all thoughts of celebrities and masterclasses and film crews right out of your heads, and start on some ballet. Do you think you can manage that for me?"

"Yes, Ms Wells," the class chorused.

The girls all went over to take their positions at the barre, but nobody could help smiling excitedly to one another about the amazing news.

"I knew this was going to be a good term," Ellie whispered to Grace as they took their places at the barre, "but I never dreamed it was going to be this exciting!"

That evening, as soon as they'd finished dinner, Ellie announced that she couldn't wait any longer to e-mail Heather, her best friend from Chicago, with the news. "Even Heather has heard of Lim Soo May and Christopher Blackwell," she said to her friends. "And Heather is so *not* a bunhead!"

Lara giggled. "Bunhead" was the word that the students used to describe somebody who lived and breathed ballet. "I'm going to be even more of a bunhead if it means a chance to be taught by Lim Soo May," she vowed. "In fact, I'm going to go off to the practice studio right now. Anybody else coming?"

"Of course!" Belle said, grabbing her ballet shoes at once.

"Me too," Grace said, jumping up too.

Bryony and Naomi decided to join them, but Kate mumbled something about her homework and buried her nose in her book.

Ellie cast a curious look at Kate. It wasn't like Kate to refuse extra practice – usually she was hard-working and totally dedicated to her dancing. Right now, though, she seemed to be the only one of them who *didn't* seem enthralled by the idea of the famous dancers' visit.

As she left the dorm, Ellie wondered if Kate

was brooding about whatever it was that the head of Lower School had said to her the day before. What could Miss Purvis have told her?

Down in the computer room, Ellie fired off an excited e-mail to Heather, telling her all about her wonderful news. She and Heather had been inseparable back in Chicago and even though she'd made so many new friends in England, Ellie still liked to e-mail Heather as often as possible, to catch up.

Ellie was just about to e-mail her Oxford friends, Bethany and Phoebe, with the same news when a return e-mail from Heather pinged right back into her inbox. Excellent! Heather was online, too!

You're not the only one with awesome news, Heather had written. *You'll never guess who's going to be flying into London this weekend...*

Who? Ellie typed back at once.

Yours truly! Heather replied. *I'm coming over on an exchange programme to Paris! It was so popular that I didn't get picked originally – but a couple of guys had to drop out, and I was on the waiting list. So now I get to go instead!! I am really excited – French is my favourite subject at school and I can't believe I'm actually going to be speaking the language for real, in Paris, France!*

We all fly over to London on Friday – yep, THIS Friday! – and then stay in a hostel for the weekend before travelling to Paris on Monday. So, I was wondering, girlfriend, if you're free to meet up somewhere this weekend?!

Ellie blinked in disbelief at Heather's message and promptly read it all over again just to make sure she hadn't imagined it. She hadn't. Wow – Heather in London! How much fun was that going to be?

I am TOTALLY free to meet up this weekend! Ellie typed back. Her fingers could hardly type quickly enough, she was so delighted. *I'll have to see if Mum is free to come down and bring me to meet you though – we're not allowed to go out* of school on our own. *She just HAS to be! Watch this space!*

Heather's reply came back almost instantly. *No need – I've already been in touch with her!* Ellie read. She blinked in surprise, and read on. *I e-mailed your mum first to see if she was free this weekend – and she said yes! It's all arranged, Ellie – we're going to see each other again in just three days! Oh, and you'd better schedule me in for the weekend three weeks after that, too – we're all stopping off in London again for a few days before flying home. Awesome, huh?*

Ellie's eyes goggled at the words. What an unbelievable surprise! *You are a superstar,* she typed back, feeling choked at the thought of Heather sorting everything out for them. *I so can't wait to see you again!*

Me too, Heather wrote back. *Bring on Saturday!!*

Ellie couldn't stop grinning as they said their cyber-goodbyes. She was just *thrilled* at the thought of seeing Heather again. It had been almost two years since they'd been together. Letters and e-mails were nice, but they weren't anything near as good as actually hanging out.

She quickly e-mailed her mum, *Just heard from Heather — thank you! Thank you! Thank you!* Then, still smiling a Cheshire Cat smile, Ellie logged off and rushed to tell her school friends all about Heather's trip.

Dear Diary,

I can't believe that this term has only just begun — there are already so many exciting things lined up! First the chance to be coached by Lim Soo May — what a terrifying/exciting opportunity! Please PLEASE let her pick me for her masterclass! There are only three places up for grabs and I am already willing to put in hours and hours of practice plus gallons of blood, sweat and tears at the thought. I can hardly imagine how amazing it would be to have a masterclass from an international superstar. Wow, wow, and triple wow. We are not worthy, etc.!

If that wasn't enough, I just heard that Heather's going to be in London this weekend. How good is that??! It's been so long since we were last together, I can't believe I'm actually going to see her again, here in England. I bet it's going to be just like it was before — best friends for ever!

Chapter Three

"Phew! That was hard work!" Ellie sighed. "I thought that series of *sissonnes* was never going to end."

It was Friday morning, and she and her friends were up in the dorm, getting dressed after their post-ballet class showers. Much as Ellie loved ballet, it seemed as if Ms Wells was driving them very hard in preparation for Lim Soo May's forthcoming visit.

"Those *ballonnés*, too," Lara groaned, massaging her calves before pulling on her socks. "All that bouncing made me feel like Tigger."

"I don't know about that," Naomi said,

combing her hair. "It just made me feel like lying down."

Mrs Hall put her head around the dorm door at that moment. "Hello, girls. Is Kate in here?" she wanted to know.

Kate, who was putting on her shoes, waved. "Over here," she called.

Mrs Hall stepped into the dorm – and as she did so, a gasp went around the room. "These have arrived for you," Mrs Hall said, with a smile. She was holding an enormous bouquet of flowers – pale pink roses, creamy white lilies, and shocking pink tulips arranged with lots of luscious green foliage.

Ellie watched curiously as Kate promptly turned scarlet and went over to collect the flowers, with her head down. *Did somebody send flowers to Kate to cheer her up?* she wondered. She'd been so quiet all week, after all.

"I've put them in a vase for you," Mrs Hall said, handing it over carefully. "They'll need to go in the common room once you've finished admiring them, as I don't think there'll be enough room near your bed. Aren't they beautiful, though? Those lilies smell wonderful."

To Ellie's surprise, Kate wasn't looking particularly thrilled by this unexpected gift. "Um . . . yes. Thank you," Kate mumbled.

"Oh, and there's a card here too," Mrs Hall added, passing a small white envelope to Kate. "Lucky girl. I wish somebody would send *me* flowers like that."

Ellie and the other girls watched as Kate carried the flowers over to her part of the dorm and plonked them down on her bedside table without a second look. She opened the card, scanned it briefly, and turned it face down beside the flowers. Then she went back to dressing herself as if nothing unusual had just happened.

"Well, go on, tell us who they're from!"

Lara cried impatiently. She went over to smell the flowers. "It's not your birthday, is it, Kate?"

"No," Kate replied shortly, pulling her on her blouse.

"That's right, you're a Gemini Junebug, aren't you?" Naomi said. She too was walking over to have a closer look at the flowers. "So who are they from?" she added. Before Kate could reply, Naomi had picked up the card. "To my darling Kate – can't wait to see you!" she read aloud, raising her eyebrows. "Darling Kate, eh? Who's sent you such gorgeous flowers, then, darling Kate?"

Kate tucked her blouse into her skirt and started brushing out her hair with long vigorous strokes. "Oh, nobody very interesting," she said, staring at the floor. Her cheeks were still scarlet and Ellie thought she seemed a little annoyed at all the questions. But what did she expect? It wasn't like any of them got flowers out of the blue like this. Of *course* they were all dying to know what was going on!

Kate stuffed her pencil case and diary into a bag, and then took hold of the vase of flowers. It was so full, Ellie could barely see Kate's face over the top of all the foliage. "Right. Time for art," Kate said abruptly. "See you guys in there." And, whirling around, she whisked the flowers to the common room.

Ellie gazed after her. "Why wouldn't she tell us who the flowers were from?" she wondered aloud.

"It must be somebody with a lot of money," Belle pointed out, her big brown eyes thoughtful. "Flowers like that are *not* cheap, I'm sure."

Grace nodded. "I don't get why she couldn't tell us who sent them, though," she said.

"Don't you?" Naomi said, hopping from one foot to the next. "*I* do; it must be a secret boyfriend. It's got to be! Who else would do such a romantic thing?"

"It would explain why she was being all secretive about them," Lara said, nodding. "Hey, and do you remember how funny she was on Sunday when we were teasing her about having a boyfriend?"

"And there was that phone call that she slunk off to take," Ellie remembered. "Like it was some big secret."

"Oh, yes!" Belle said. "I'd forgotten that. She was really shifty about it, wasn't she?" Then her eyes sparkled. "Ooh, do you think it's somebody in the school?"

"I saw her talking to William Forrest the other day, you know, that blond boy in Year 8," Bryony put in excitedly.

"But she told me that she thought Richard Harper was the tastiest boy in Year 8," Lara added. "So it might be him."

"Or there's that boy in Year 9, Alex, who

lives in Newcastle, like Kate," Ellie remembered. "Maybe they were hanging out together over the vacation."

"Ooh, how exciting!" Naomi said, rubbing her hands together. "I'll have to consult my tarot cards to see what they say about this."

Ellie laughed as Naomi immediately produced a pack of cards, along with a book describing the card meanings. "Any excuse," she said. "OK, then, Madame Naomi – tell us what's happening with Kate."

"Let's see," Naomi began. "We need a card to represent Kate first." She consulted her book. "I'd say she's probably the Princess of Wands: *a youthful, free-spirited individual. . .*" she read aloud. "Yep, that sounds like our Kate."

She shuffled through the cards to find the right one. "Here we go." She laid the card down on her bed. "Now, I'll just shuffle up the others and see what comes out. Obviously

Kate should really be shuffling the cards, but as she's not here, I'll have to do my best."

Ellie went nearer to watch, as did Lara, Belle and Bryony.

"You're going to be late for art with all this mumbo-jumbo," Grace warned, gathering up her art things.

"I'll just be a minute," Naomi said, dealing a series of cards out in a pattern, face down. She turned the first one over. "Right. . . So this is Kate's past. The Three of Fire." She consulted her book. "Nice card. It can mean creative energy. . ."

"Wow," Bryony said, leaning over for a closer look. "That is so accurate! Creative energy – well, that sums ballet up perfectly!"

"I know. Spooky," Naomi said, and then she looked over at Grace. "The power of the tarot should be respected by everyone," she said, lowering her voice mysteriously. She turned over another card and laid it face up. "And Kate's present card is. . ."

Then she giggled. "The Two of Water! I knew it!" she exclaimed, flipping through her book. "Yes. An emotional connection between two people. . ." she read. "And I quote: 'Can mean a love affair or a holiday romance'!"

There was a silence as everybody stared at the cards on Naomi's bed.

"I am – how would you say it? – spooked," Belle confessed. "You truly are Madame Naomi!"

Naomi bowed dramatically and then shut her tarot book with a loud bang. "Kate Walker – we've got your number, buddy," she said.

"Wait a minute. If there *is* something going on with William or Richard or Alex, why would they send flowers when they're here in the same school as Kate?" Grace countered. "It's a bit over the top, isn't it? Not to mention expensive."

Naomi shrugged. "Well, maybe they just wanted to impress her. After all, when you're in loooooove, nothing's too over the top, is it?" she reasoned. "Or so I've heard anyway. What would I know? Nobody's fallen in love with me and sent *me* flowers . . . yet! Now for the future card. . ."

"I wonder what this one is going to mean," Belle said excitedly.

"It means we're going to be late," Grace put in, tapping her foot impatiently. "Look at the time!"

Ellie glanced at her watch and yelled in alarm. "You're right, Grace! The future card will just have to wait. But I can predict this much: Mr Phillips isn't going to love us much today – because we really *are* all going to be late for art!"

As Ellie and her friends went down the steps and rushed to the art room, her mind was racing just as fast as her feet. Never mind the tarot cards, Ellie just wished that Kate felt able to talk about what was happening with her. Surely they were all good enough friends for Kate to be able to confide in one of them at least? What was with all the secrets?

"Ahh, there you are," Mr Phillips's voice boomed out as they arrived at the art room at last. "I was starting to think half my class had gone down with some mystery illness." His smile reassured them that he was only joking.

Mr Phillips is one of the nicest teachers at The Royal Ballet School, Ellie thought.

"Now, cast your minds back, all of you," he said, once Ellie and her friends had sat down. "Back, way back, back through the mists of time. . . Well, to the end of last term, at least." A chuckle went around the room. "We never *quite* finished our masks, did we?" Mr Phillips asked.

"No, sir," a few of the students replied.

Ellie loved the way that so many of her academic classes related to ballet in some way or other. In maths, for example, they often looked at puzzles in terms of ballerinas or dance steps. In music, they studied different scores from various ballets. And last term in their art class, they had looked at designs for costumes and theatre sets for different ballets. They'd discussed how each ballet had a different mood and atmosphere, and how this needed to be reflected in its theatrical design. The last part of the project had been to each make a costume mask for fun, but time had run out before they'd all completed them.

"I thought you could finish your masks this morning and then spend a few minutes at the end of the class taking it in turns to talk through your work with the rest of the class," Mr Phillips announced. "How you made it, why you chose that particular design, and so on." He waved his arm to a long wide table on the far side of the room. "Your masks have been set out over there, so help yourselves – and get cracking!"

Ellie and Grace went over to collect their masks together. Ellie's mask was pale pink and edged in a gorgeous crimson ribbon. She'd spent a very long time cutting out tiny pink paper ballet shoes that she was going to hang from the edges of the mask, like tassels.

Grace's mask was a light green colour, half-covered with small tissue-paper flowers. She looked at it critically as they sat down at the table again. "It's funny how your memory plays tricks on you, isn't it?" she said to the others. She poked at her mask rather dolefully. "I remembered this being really pretty – and almost finished, too. Now I come back to see it looks like something a five year old would make – and it's nowhere *near* finished!"

"It's beautiful, Grace," Ellie assured her

perfectionist friend. "I'm almost finished, so I'll help you when I'm done."

Naomi glued on some pink feathers at the side of her mask and then promptly sneezed them off again. "Achoo! Achoo!" She wiped her eyes, which were rapidly turning red, then pulled a face. "Oh, no! I think I'm allergic to my own mask!"

"You would be!" Bryony giggled.

Lara was sorting through a box of odds and ends, picking out sequins for her silvery mask. She tossed Naomi two enormous pink sparkly stars. "Here – glue these on instead," she joked. "With a bit of luck, they might even hide your face."

"Thanks for your help, but I couldn't deprive the world of my gorgeousness, Lara," Naomi said, batting her eyelashes. "It would be too cruel!"

Ellie started tying lengths of silver thread around her tiny ballet shoes, ready to glue them on. "How's yours coming along, Kate?" she asked conversationally.

Kate was sticking on a fringe of curled eyelashes around the eyeholes of a black cat mask. "Almost there," she replied, pressing the eyelashes carefully into place. Then she stared at it. "Oops. Do cats actually *have* eyelashes?" she asked.

"Nope," Naomi said. "Hey, I'll swap you some eyelashes for some feathers."

Kate wrinkled her nose. "It's a *cat*, not a parakeet," she told Naomi. "What self-respecting cat would wear pink feathers?"

Lara looked over. "How about using those eyelashes as very short whiskers instead?" she suggested.

Now it was Kate's turn to giggle as she unpeeled her cat's eyelashes and tried them for size on the cat's cheeks. "Hmmm. . . Maybe not," she said. "They look more like caterpillars than cat whiskers!"

Ellie tossed her a packet of pipe cleaners, pleased to see Kate smiling for a change. "Here, these might do the trick," she said.

"Has everybody finished?" Mr Phillips said, making Ellie jump.

"Um. . . Not quite!" the girls at Ellie's table called out together.

"Five more minutes, then," Mr Phillips told them. "And then it's time to show us your creations!"

The five minutes passed by very quickly. Ellie couldn't believe it when Mr Phillips clapped his hands and told them that time was up. "Now we'll go around the classroom and each of you can stand up with your mask and tell us about it," he said. He looked at Naomi, who was now proudly wearing her finished mask, and smiled. "Yes, Naomi, if wearing your mask makes you happy, then go ahead, but nobody else has to, obviously. Perhaps you'd like to go first?"

Naomi, of course, needed no further encouragement. She leaped to her feet at once. "Achoo!" She sneezed, making everybody giggle. She took her mask off again reluctantly. "And it's so darn gorgeous too," she sighed. "Trust me to make something I can't actually wear!"

She held up her flamboyant feathered creation so that the whole class could see it. "This was inspired by a carnival I went to, last summer, in Manchester," she said. "There was a big parade through the city with floats, and loads of people were dressed up. My favourite float was one called 'Carnival Queens', and everyone on it was wearing feather boas and gorgeous glamorous dresses and high heels. For me, dressing up is like becoming a completely different person. You put on a costume and you become somebody else. I guess a mask can make you feel like that, too – like you're reinventing yourself, making yourself more glamorous, or more of a mystery." One of the pink feathers drifted down to the table. "Achoo!" Naomi sneezed again. She put her mask down and blew her nose. "Although I just seem to have reinvented myself as a sneezing machine," she said crossly.

Mr Phillips was smiling. "Excellent, Naomi!" he said. "You have identified two of the main uses for a mask: to reinvent yourself – and to add mystery. A mask is not just for decoration; in ballet, for instance, a dancer's mask can tell the audience something about the character they're playing. But as Naomi has said, masks can also be used to hide behind, or to hide what the wearer is thinking. Right, who's next? Grace, tell us about your mask."

Grace stood up, her cheeks turning a little pink as she held up her creation. "I got the idea when I was home one weekend," she told them. "The garden was full of spring flowers and all the colours were so beautiful together. I wanted to see if I could get the same effect on my mask. . ."

While Grace was talking, Ellie couldn't help glancing over at Kate. As had become usual lately, Kate's thoughts seemed to be elsewhere. Her eyes were down, staring at the table as she fiddled with her cat mask's pipe-cleaner whiskers.

"Thank you, Grace," Mr Phillips said once she'd finished. "Kate, your turn. Tell us about your mask. A cat mask, is it? What is it that appeals to you about cats in particular, Kate?"

Kate started as she heard her name. She got to her feet and cleared her throat. "My grandmother has a black cat like this called Sheba," she began. "I spend ages just watching her. I love how independent she is. Cats do things their own way, don't they? I like that." She hesitated for a moment. "And that's how *I* want to be. . ." she said slowly. "It's really important to me to be independent – you know, stand on my own two feet."

"Or your own *four* feet if you're wearing your cat mask," Mr Phillips joked. "Thank you, Kate. Very interesting," he said. "Another good example of using a mask to say something about a character. Belle, tell us about your mask."

Belle started telling the class about the mask she had made. But Ellie couldn't stop her glance from returning to Kate, who was now staring blankly ahead, lost in thought again. It was almost as if she were wearing a kind of invisible mask right now – to cover up any clue to what she might be thinking. Just what was going on with her lately?

Dear Diary,
The plot thickens! I'm curled up on a beanbag in the common room and all I can smell is the

lilies and roses from Kate's bouquet. They are absolutely heavenly, but Kate's acting as if they don't exist. We're still no closer to finding out who sent them. I wonder why Kate won't tell us? All this mystery is driving me nuts!!

Hey, I've just thought of something... What if Kate really has started going out with someone here at school, but she's not sure she's doing the right thing and feels guilty about it? After all, she was talking about how important her independence is to her and stuff like that in art this afternoon... Could that be why she's being so secretive? Oh, I just wish she'd confide in us!!

Speaking of art — it was a really interesting class today. Everybody's masks were so creative and different. Poor Naomi has had to take all the feathers off hers because she kept sneezing every time she went anywhere near it! She's glued on a bunch of tinsel instead — nothing subtle or plain for our Naomi...

Ooh — hot news! My mobile just beeped so I checked my messages, and there was a text message from Heather that she sent from an Internet café. I guess her mobile doesn't work over here in Europe. She's in London right now! It is so crazy that there are only a couple of miles between us — oh, I can't wait for tomorrow! I am sooo excited about hanging out with her again!

Chapter Four

Ellie thought she'd never be able to fall asleep on Friday night, she was so excited at the prospect of seeing Heather again the following morning. She lay there in bed, thinking about all the fun things she and Heather had done together back in Chicago.

The two of them had met on their very first day in kindergarten and had been inseparable ever since. Heather had lived just two blocks away from Ellie, and the two girls had played together after school at each other's houses almost every day, rain or shine.

Ellie felt a smile creep over her face as she thought about the tree house in Heather's back garden that her parents had built one summer. She and Heather had practically lived there that summer vacation, dragging up cushions and blankets, books and games, cookies and juice cartons until it felt like their own private house. And as for the fun they'd had spying on Heather's older brother, Ed...! Ellie could still remember laughing so hard she thought she was going to fall out of the tree, the time that she and Heather had spotted Ed kissing his first girlfriend when he'd thought nobody was looking.

Ellie rolled over on to her side and closed her eyes, wondering if Heather was finding it as difficult to sleep as she was. And then, before she knew it, she was opening her eyes again – and it was Saturday!

"Rise and shine!" she couldn't help yelling out cheerfully.

Lara opened one sleepy eye and squinted in Ellie's direction. "There had better be a good reason for all that shouting, Ellie Brown," she grumbled.

Ellie flung off her covers and danced her way to the showers. "There is, there *so* is!" she cried. She felt jittery with excitement, hardly able to keep still under the hot shower. She was going to see Heather, her best friend Heather, in just a few hours!

Not everybody was in such a good mood as Ellie that morning. At breakfast, Mrs Hall announced that, unfortunately, the day trip to Richmond and Kew Gardens that Naomi, Kate and Lara had signed up for had been cancelled, due to staff sickness.

"Rats," said Lara, stirring her porridge. "I really wanted to do some shopping this morning, too. All my cousins seem to have their birthdays around now, and I've got about ninety-eight presents and cards to get."

"And I was looking forward to a hot

chocolate with marshmallows at our favourite café," Naomi grumbled. "Not to mention a wedge of fudge cake. What are we going to do now?"

That was when Ellie had a genius idea. "Hey, why don't you guys come into London with me and my mum?" she suggested. "We've arranged to meet my friend Heather at a coffee shop at Covent Garden – Naomi, you can get your hot chocolate and fudge cake fix there. And Lara, you can do some shopping afterwards." She clapped her hands excitedly. "I know you'll love Heather! And where's Kate? She might want to come too!" Grace, Belle and Bryony already had other weekend plans.

"Count me in!" Naomi said like a shot. "Are you sure your mum won't mind chaperoning three extra bunheads, though, Ellie? It's too short notice, isn't it?"

"I'm sure she won't mind," Ellie said

happily. "The more the merrier! But you'll need to get permission, I think. Mrs Hall won't let you go without it."

Lara nodded. "We'll just have to phone our mums and get them to call Mrs Hall, saying they're happy for us to go," she added.

Naomi grinned and whipped out her mobile. "Well, what are we waiting for?"

While her friends took turns using Naomi's phone, Ellie looked around for Kate. Privately, she thought that a fun day out was exactly what Kate needed right now. It might snap her out of her strange mood.

She spotted Kate deep in conversation with a boy in the canteen line. "Kate!" she called, running up to her. "Since the Richmond trip has been cancelled, Lara and Naomi are calling their mums to see if they can come with me and my mum to the West End. What do you think? Do you want to come, too?"

Kate blinked, as if she hadn't been listening.

"The West End?" she repeated. Then she smiled. "Sounds fun. Yes, please! Count me in. I'll get permission."

Ellie went back to her friends as Kate carried on her conversation. Good! So that was Lara, Naomi and Kate. . .

"What were those two talking about?" Lara hissed to Ellie across the table as she sat down again. "Kate and William Forrest, I mean?"

Ellie glanced over to where Kate was still chatting with the boy, near the cereal boxes. "I didn't listen. Why?" she asked curiously.

"Keep up, Ellie!" Naomi groaned. "Honestly, I know you're excited about today, but you shouldn't let your gossip radar slip for a second! We were just wondering if it was *William* who sent Kate the flowers."

Ellie's eyes widened. "Oh, I see!" she exclaimed as she suddenly remembered. "Bryony saw Kate with William the other day too, didn't she?"

Bryony nodded, and Lara lowered her eyebrows at Ellie, pretending to frown. "Sure, Ellie Brown, you'll never make a super-sleuth," she said.

Ellie gave a sheepish grin. "Sorry, I was so excited about my fantastic idea that I just interrupted them without paying any attention to what they were talking about."

"Well, whatever is going on, you'd better not stare so obviously," Grace put in. She shrugged. "Anyway, for all we know, they could just be discussing what cereal to have for breakfast."

"Right, Grace," Lara said, deadpan. "Because breakfast cereal is such an exciting topic of conversation – I don't think so!"

Ellie spooned in some of her porridge thoughtfully. *Kate and William Forrest, an item?* Well, stranger things had happened at The Royal Ballet School.

"Do you think we should ask her about it?"

Belle wondered, her dark eyes locked curiously on Kate.

Ellie shook her head. "Better not. She'll tell us in her own time," she said. She stirred her oatmeal and added a little more sugar. Or at least she *hoped* Kate would confide in them. . .

An hour or so later, with the blessing of their mums and Mrs Hall, Ellie and her friends were catching the train from Richmond into central London with Ellie's mum. The plan was to meet Heather in Covent Garden, at a coffee shop right next to the hostel where the exchange·group was staying. They would have most of the day together before Heather had to be back with her school group at five o'clock to get ready for their evening meal out together.

By the time they'd caught the tube into Covent Garden, Ellie was starting to feel breathless with excitement. Would Heather look the same, she wondered? Would Ellie even *recognize* her, after all this time?

Ellie needn't have worried. As soon as they entered the coffee shop just down from Covent Garden station, she caught sight of Heather's unruly chestnut curls. A big grin spread across her face and then she was running towards her old friend. "Heather!" she cried happily, and then, seconds later, the two girls were hugging each other.

"Your hair got so long!" exclaimed Heather, pulling back to examine Ellie.

"And yours is as amazing as ever!" Ellie said with a grin, looping one of the chestnut ringlets with her finger.

"I love your coat," Heather said, and then hugged her again. "Wow, isn't this awesome? I am so psyched about us hanging out again!"

"I know," Ellie said joyfully. "My mum's here, too, of course. Oh, and. . ." she waved a hand behind her to where her friends were standing. "Some of the girls from school are here, as well. You don't mind, do you? Mrs Hall – that's our housemother – told us this morning that a school trip had been cancelled and suddenly everybody had nothing to do. . ." Ellie broke off, suddenly out of breath. "Come and say hello to Heather, everyone!"

Ellie's mum came forward and hugged Heather warmly. "Oh, it's like having my other daughter back again," she joked. "I think I've missed you almost as much as Ellie has, Heather. How was your flight? What do you think of London?"

"Awesome, and awesome," Heather replied, grinning. "It's good to see you, too. My mum said to say hi. Oh, and Mrs Foster from number seventy-two sent her best wishes. . ."

"Heather, this is Naomi, Lara and Kate," Ellie said, introducing each of them in turn. She felt proud of her friends as she pointed them out to Heather. Who would have thought it – Heather, meeting some of her Royal Ballet School friends? It was like two worlds coming together.

"Hi," Heather said. "Nice to meet you all. I've heard lots about you."

"All good, I hope?" Naomi asked, raising her eyebrows mock-suspiciously at Ellie. "Now, do we have time for a hot chocolate here?" She grinned in a friendly way at Heather. "Got to get my Saturday fix. Hope you don't mind."

"Sure," Heather replied politely.

"Great!" Naomi beamed. "Let's find a table."

"I've made a little list, Ell. . ." Heather said, when they'd all placed their orders. She held up a piece of paper and smiled at Ellie. "Three weeks' worth of sightseeing packed into one day. I hope that's OK. There's just so much I want to see in London!"

"No problem," Ellie replied, taking the

paper from her friend and scanning it. "National Gallery, Oxford Street, Buckingham Palace. . ." She read down the rest of the list and nodded. "But we can't leave Covent Garden without showing you where The Royal Ballet Upper School is – and the Bridge of Aspiration, of course. They're just around the corner!"

"OK," Heather said, tucking an arm into Ellie's as they walked to the table. "I can't wait."

Naomi was making them all laugh so much with her impressions of the coffee shop's surly waiter! Although Heather had grown a little quiet, Ellie noticed. *It must be jet lag*, she thought. *Poor Heather!* She remembered how tired she and her mum had been the first time they'd flown to Britain from Chicago.

Heather glanced at her watch. "Could we get going soon, you think?" she asked Ellie in a low voice.

Ellie looked down at her own watch. A whole hour had gone by! "Oh, yes!" she replied. "How did that happen? Come on, guys," she said to the others. "We need to move."

Coming out on to the busy cobblestone street, Ellie led the way through the stream of shoppers and audiences circling the colourful street performers. She turned the corner into Floral Street, where the entrance to The Royal Ballet Upper School faced the Royal Opera House. The two buildings were joined together by the spectacular Bridge of Aspiration.

And there it was – stretched across the street high above their heads – a twisted tunnel of glass and aluminium, glittering in the sunlight.

"Wow, that *is* cool!" Heather breathed. "But why is it called the Bridge of Aspiration?"

"It links The Royal Ballet Upper School with The Royal Ballet studios inside the Royal Opera House," Ellie explained proudly. As they walked under the bridge, Ellie pointed to the glass-fronted entrance of the Upper School. "Most of The Royal Ballet Lower School students dream of coming here when they get older – and then crossing the bridge to dance as a member of The Royal Ballet. It's what we all aspire to."

Heather smiled and gave Ellie's arm a squeeze. "You'll get there, I know you will," she whispered.

Ellie's mum was looking at her map. "What do you say we go to the National Gallery now, guys? It's in Trafalgar Square, Heather, which isn't too far for us to walk."

"Actually, before we start on the sights, would anybody mind if we just pop into the Royal Opera House for two minutes?" Lara asked. "I won't be long; I just want to pick up one of their summer programmes, to see what shows are coming on."

Mrs Brown smiled. "Fine by me, if Heather doesn't mind?"

"Um . . . OK, I guess," Heather said.

She sounded a little doubtful, so Ellie took her arm. "Come on," she said, leading her friend to the Royal Opera House. "You're gonna love it. Remember I wrote to you about me dancing on the stage there at Christmas, Heather? It's just the most gorgeous building – definitely worth a few photos." She grinned happily. "And your exchange teachers will be so impressed that you've been inside such a cultural landmark."

The Royal Opera House is truly wonderful, Ellie thought as they stepped into the beautiful old stone building. It was the home of The Royal Ballet and suitably impressive with its mix of old and contemporary architecture.

"Hey, look!"

Naomi's excited voice broke into Ellie's thoughts as they entered the foyer. Ellie turned to see where Naomi was pointing, and her eyes fell upon a life-size poster that was up for a forthcoming production of *Romeo and Juliet* . . . starring none other than Lim Soo May and Christopher Blackwell.

"Ohmigosh!" Ellie cried, dragging Heather over with her for a closer look. "I told you they were coming to our school, didn't I? Wow. Doesn't Lim Soo May look fantastic in that costume? She is so beautiful!"

"I didn't know they were dancing *Romeo and Juliet* together," said Naomi excitedly. "What perfect casting!"

"We can ask her all about it when she comes to school," said Lara, gazing at the poster. "Wow. I can't believe we're going to meet them soon."

"We might even be able to persuade Mrs Hall to arrange a school trip to see this production!" Ellie suggested, dancing on the spot.

"I just cannot wait to meet Lim Soo May!" Naomi cried, clasping her hands together. She pretended to address the figures in the poster, wagging her finger at them. "Now, you must choose *me* for your masterclass, do you hear? Me – Naomi Crawford! Remember that name, please!"

Lara and Ellie got into the spirit of things and started begging the picture of Lim Soo May to choose them as well. And then Ellie noticed that Kate wasn't joining in. In fact she was looking distinctly uncomfortable.

"Oh, come on, you lot, what's the big deal?" Kate burst out suddenly. "She's only a person, it's not like she's a . . . a *goddess*, or something!"

There was a stunned silence, and then Kate took a deep breath and went on. "I'm sick of everyone going on and on about them. I hate all that celebrity nonsense." She hoisted her shoulder bag higher up and turned on her heel. "I'll wait for you guys outside. I thought we were meant to be going sightseeing and shopping, not gossiping all day!"

Ellie and her friends gazed after Kate in amazement.

Heather turned to Ellie. "What's that all about?" she whispered uneasily.

Ellie shrugged. "No idea," she confessed. "She's just been acting kind of strange lately. I don't know why."

"Well, Kate has got a point," Ellie's mum said briskly. "Poor Heather's been waiting for ever to go to the National Gallery. Should we head over there now?"

"Sure," Ellie said. "Sorry, Heather. Let's go and see some art." She couldn't help wondering about Kate's outburst, though. What on earth had sparked *that* off?

* * *

"Phew! My feet are killing me!" Ellie groaned. "Talk about shop till you drop."

"I'm dropping, I'm dropping," Naomi moaned in agreement. "Why on earth did I wear these new sandals for a day of sightseeing? Am I completely crazy? I'll never be able to dance again with all my blisters!"

It was five o'clock, and time for Heather to be back at her hostel with the rest of her group. Ellie and her friends had been around the National Gallery and had lunch in an Italian restaurant nearby, then hit the shops in Oxford Street. To The Royal Ballet School girls' delight, they'd found a dance shop near Oxford Street, and had whiled away a good hour and a half in there, trying on gorgeous spangly tutus and new leotards. Unfortunately this had meant that they hadn't managed to see all the sights on Heather's list. Heather had been a little quiet in the dance shop, even when Naomi had waltzed around wearing a green feathered outfit that had had all of the others in fits of giggles. Ellie had put it down to jet lag again – and tiredness too, probably, from all of their pavement-pounding.

"Today's gone so quickly," Heather said. "Thanks for taking us around, Amy," she said to Ellie's mum, hugging her goodbye. Then she turned to Ellie. "Um. . . Nice to see you, Ellie. Bye."

Heather was about to go when Ellie pulled her back in surprise. "Hey – you forgot *my* hug!" she laughed.

"Oh, yeah. Bye, Ellie." Heather put her arms around Ellie, but Ellie couldn't help feeling that the embrace was rather stiff and uncomfortable.

"Are you OK?" Ellie asked in a low voice, wondering what was wrong with her friend.

Heather looked pale as she stepped away. "Sure. Better go. Bye, everybody," she said, not meeting Ellie's eye. She turned towards the hostel's entrance.

"Have a great time in Paris!" Ellie yelled after her. "And I'll see you in three weeks!"

Lara and Kate added their goodbyes in a chorus.

"*Au revoir*," Naomi cried, and did a few high kicks for good measure that got everybody giggling again.

But Heather didn't seem to hear them, or notice Naomi's display. She'd caught sight of her French teacher and the rest of her exchange group in the hostel foyer, and was hurrying over to meet them, as arranged.

"We'd better go, too," Ellie's mum said. "I promised Mrs Hall I'd have you back by six o'clock."

Before Ellie followed her friends back towards the tube station, she glanced over her shoulder to see if Heather would turn and give her a last wave. But she was deep in conversation with another girl, and she never looked back.

Dear Diary,

Heather seemed a little bit distant with me when we said goodbye this afternoon, I don't know why. I feel a little disappointed. I was really excited to see her, too. I guess I was just expecting us to click straight back into being how we were together in Chicago – but it didn't turn out to be that easy.

She's probably still getting over her jet lag. I hope that's all. I hope it's not because she's decided she doesn't like me any more. That's just too awful to even think about!

I wish I could e-mail her to find out if there is anything wrong, but I've got no way of getting in touch with her now that she's on her way to France. I'll just have to talk to her about it when she's back in London, I guess.

First Kate goes all weird on us, and now Heather! Why can't everyone stay the same? Kate hasn't said much since her outburst in the Royal Opera House. In fact, I haven't seen her much at all this evening. Naomi said she saw her sneaking out to make a phone call earlier, but that was hours ago. I wonder if she's ever going to let us in on her secret?

Chapter Five

The next day was Sunday. Ellie lay on her bed in the dorm after breakfast, not feeling very much like starting her maths homework. She was in a strange mood; she hadn't yet been able to shake off her feelings of unease at how things had been with Heather the day before. It wasn't that she hadn't enjoyed seeing her old friend, it was more that –

"Ellie! Ellie!"

It was Naomi's voice. Ellie rolled over to see her friend standing in the doorway, a ping-pong racket in her hand.

"Come on, we need you!" Naomi told her, rather bossily. "Lara, Kate, you too. I've arranged a table tennis tournament –

girls against boys. Are you up for it?"

Ellie sat up and swung her legs off her bed. "Sounds good to me," she said thankfully. "A million times better than maths homework, that's for sure." Lying there brooding wasn't making her feel any better, but table tennis might just do the trick.

Lara got up as well, but Kate stayed put. "I'm not really in the mood," she said, not looking up from the school book she was reading.

"What, but you're in the mood for homework?" joked Naomi. She pretended to call out of the door. "Send for a doctor! Kate Walker has finally lost her marbles!"

Kate blushed. "No, I'm going to write some letters in a minute," she replied.

"Come on, Kate," Lara wheedled. "We know you're the best at table tennis. Don't you want to help the girls storm to victory?"

Kate shook her head. "Not really," she said, not looking up.

Ellie, Lara and Naomi exchanged glances but none of them pushed Kate any further. "Letters to write, eh?" Naomi said, melodramatically, as they left the dorm. "Letters to *whom*, I wonder?"

"Are you thinking what I'm thinking, girls?" Lara asked, raising her eyebrows comically. "*Love* letters?"

"Exactly," Naomi said. "Why else would she want to miss my table tennis tournament, eh? It must be something *really* serious!"

Downstairs, Ellie laughed when she saw that Naomi had roped in just about everybody in Year 7 who was left in school.

"Right," Naomi said, clapping her hands for silence. "Let's see. We've got . . . eight girls and . . . nine boys." She glanced at Ellie and Lara, and they both knew what she was thinking. The girls needed Kate!

Naomi shrugged though and just grinned at

the boys. "Not to worry. You guys probably need an extra player, seeing as we girls are so much better than you, am I right?"

"You are so wrong, Ms Crawford," Matt grinned back. "I give you ten minutes, girls, before you're begging us to let you win a couple of games."

"Fighting talk!" laughed Ellie. "We'll see about that, Matt Haslum."

Naomi explained the rules. The girls would line up on one side of the table, the boys on the other. "We take it in turns to have five shots each before passing the racket back to the next player," Naomi said. "And, just to make it a bit more interesting, we could add a few extra rules."

"Like what?" Justin wanted to know.

"Like . . . you have to do a *pirouette* between each shot," Naomi said, her eyes twinkling. "Are you up for it?"

Ellie laughed and nodded. This sounded

like it was going to be the funniest game of table tennis she'd ever played!

"OK, then," Naomi said. "Let's get going."

Everybody lined up to play. Naomi was the first in the line of girls, and Matt was the first boy. Before long, they were giggling breathlessly as they tried to maintain the game, while spinning around between shots. Somehow or other, they both managed to keep the ball in play, but their shots were getting wilder and wilder, with both players having to lunge frantically to send the ball back each time.

"Phew," gasped Naomi as her five shots were up and she thrust the racket into Ellie's hand. "I'm exhausted!"

Now it was Ellie's turn, and Toby was on the boys' side. *Whack!* Ellie hit the ball dead centre across the net, and whizzed around on the toe of her trainer. Help! The ball was already coming right back at her and she felt way off balance! She stretched out desperately with her bat to send it bouncing back to Toby and spun around for the wobbliest *pirouette* she'd ever done.

Across the table, Toby had managed to trip on his trainer lace and was laughing on the floor, holding the ball in his left hand. "I caught it at least," he said, getting back to his feet. "Is that worth anything?"

"Certainly not," Lara told him. "It's table tennis, not cricket! That's one point to the girls. Ellie, your serve."

After an hour or so, everybody was out of breath and absolutely worn out. Somebody had suggested a new rule every so often so that instead of doing a *pirouette* between shots, they had to touch their toes between shots, or *jeté*, or run to touch the wall.

"That was crazy," Belle panted, tucking a stray hair into place as they made their way back to the dorm. "You girls are just —" She held up her hands – "quite mad!" She grinned before anybody could protest. "But nice mad. Very funny mad. My friends in France wouldn't believe the game we just had."

"And we won!" Ellie cheered. "Victory to the 'nice mad, funny mad' girls!"

"We won by a mile, too," Lara panted, grinning happily. "A landslide. That was an excellent idea, Naomi. We must –"

Lara's voice broke off as she pushed open the dorm door. Kate was in there, talking on her mobile, looking and sounding furious.

"Of *course* I miss you," she snapped, "but I've told you before – it's difficult for me to be seen with you at school."

Lara stepped back into the hallway, an awkward expression on her face. "Um . . . maybe we should let Kate have a bit of privacy," she said.

"Perhaps we could get a cold drink," Belle

said, fanning her cheeks with a hand. "I am very hot after our game."

"Good idea," Ellie said. "We can get a drink and go and sit outside somewhere."

Naomi was looking torn. "Or we could just . . . listen in for a while?" she suggested, only half-joking.

"Come on, Miss Nosy," Ellie said, dragging her friend along. "Quit flapping those great elephant ears, and let's go outside."

"I'd better just get my purse. . ." Naomi said, trying to dodge back into the dorm.

"No, you don't," Lara said, pulling her away. "Naomi, stop trying to eavesdrop! I'll buy you a drink!"

Naomi laughed. "OK, OK," she said. "You caught me. But hey, you can't blame me for trying. I'm dying to know what's going on."

"Where's your crystal ball when you need it?" Ellie joked. "I thought Madame Naomi knew everything!"

The girls went back downstairs to the canteen. Then, cold drinks in hand, they went out into the school gardens and stretched out on the grass.

"That's better," Ellie said, enjoying the feeling of sunshine on her skin as she sipped her juice. "Bliss."

"I wonder who Kate was talking to in there?" Naomi said. "She sounded really angry, didn't she?"

"I've never seen Kate like that before," Bryony added, sipping her drink.

"Nor me," Ellie agreed. "Kate's usually really . . . I don't know . . . in control, I guess."

Naomi sat up suddenly, her eyes wide. "Of course!" she cried. "It's got to be her secret boyfriend! The one who sent her flowers on Friday! The one she was writing love letters to!"

"If she's *got* a secret boyfriend," Ellie reminded Naomi. "Those flowers might have been from somebody else, like her grandma, remember."

" 'Darling Kate – I can't wait to see you!' From her *grandma*?" Naomi scoffed. "I don't think so."

"Well, a friend, then," Bryony suggested. "OK, a really good friend," she added, as Naomi gave her a disbelieving look.

"Supposing Naomi's right and Kate *is* on the phone to her secret boyfriend; then it can't be somebody in school," Lara reasoned. "Otherwise she could find him and argue with him in person."

"But did you hear what she said?" Bryony asked. "She was saying: *it's difficult for me to be seen with you at school*. So it *has* to be someone here at White Lodge! I still think it's William."

Lara didn't look so sure. "They were having a good old chat at breakfast yesterday," she said. "It wasn't too difficult to be seen with him then, was it?"

"Maybe Kate met somebody over Easter vacation," Ellie suggested. "But I'm sure she would have told us about it, if she had."

Naomi was on a roll. "Remember how far away and distracted Kate's been? She's missing her boyfriend, and that's who she was arguing with. This boy obviously doesn't want her to hide their relationship any more." Then her eyes goggled as she thought of something else. "Hey, what if he's someone rich and famous? That's why she's so secretive!"

"What, like Prince Harry?" Ellie laughed. The thought of Kate falling in love with a member of the Royal Family was beyond even Naomi's crazy ideas. "I can see it now: a child bride in the Royal Family . . . I don't think so."

"Kate's not even twelve yet, remember, Naomi," Lara pointed out. "I think Prince Harry might be just a teensy bit old for her."

"She'd look good in a tiara, though,

wouldn't she?" Ellie joked. "Princess Kate – we'd have to watch our manners, wouldn't we?"

Lara was laughing now too. "Lucky that we're all so practised at curtseying, isn't it?" she chuckled. She pretended to think. "Now, I wonder . . . which hat should I wear to the royal wedding?"

Naomi grinned. "You never know," she said, shrugging. "That could be what Miss Purvis spoke to her about last week – how the press mustn't find out, otherwise school will be besieged by journalists and paparazzi. . ." Her eyes shone. "Oh, I hope Kate *has* got a secret famous boyfriend. It would make this term even more exciting than it already is!"

Ellie called home later in the evening to thank her mum for taking them all out into London the day before.

"I'm glad you had a nice time," her mum

said. "So did I. Wasn't it fun to spend the day with Heather again?"

"Well. . ." Ellie began. She was about to say, *Well, actually, Mum, I feel a little weird about that, because. . .* But before she could begin confiding about how she was feeling, her mum started to speak again.

"In fact, it got me thinking. If Heather can go off to Paris, then I don't see why *we* can't," her mum said. "It's only a few hours away by train, after all." She paused. "So . . . we're going, Ellie!" The excitement spilled out in her voice. "*We're* going to go to Paris next weekend!"

"We're *what*?" Ellie asked, feeling stunned.

"Me and you. Steve can't get time off work, unfortunately, so it's just us two girls," her mum went on happily. "It's all arranged with school. We're going to get the Eurostar next Saturday morning, arrive in Paris around lunchtime, meet up with Heather's exchange group for a tour of Paris, then stay in a hotel that evening. Next morning, back on the train to London. How does that sound?"

"It sounds. . ." Ellie groped for words, hardly able to take it in. A week ago, she'd have jumped at the chance to spend more time with her friend – especially in Paris! A week ago, she'd have been bounding around, shrieking with excitement at this news, but now, with her new worries about her friendship with Heather, Ellie suddenly felt unsure. Would Heather *want* to see her in Paris?

"It sounds awesome," she said quickly, remembering that her mum was on the other end of the line. "Wow. You've been busy."

"I sure have. So you'd better ask Belle to teach you some extra French vocabulary, and get your overnight bag packed for next weekend!" Ellie could tell from her mum's voice that she was smiling. "I've got us some euros to spend already, and I've picked up a French phrasebook."

"Wow," Ellie said again. The news was still sinking in. "Thanks, Mum. You sure are full of surprises!"

Dear Diary,

I can't really believe it yet, but Mum's just told me that she and I are going to Paris next weekend! WOW! Paris! I'm going to Paris!

After I got off the phone with Mum, I rushed and told everyone. They're all so excited for me. Belle's been telling me all the things I'll have to do — and eat! — while I'm there. She's already started writing me a shopping list of all the different French cheeses and chocolate she wants me to bring back for her tuck box.

I still feel weird about seeing Heather again, though. Nervous, even — crazy, huh? Nervous about seeing somebody I used to be such good friends with! I just wish I could call her to check if it's OK for me and Mum to crash her Paris trip, but I've got no way of getting in touch.

I guess seeing her again next Saturday will be a chance to talk about how she feels, at least, and we can work out what went wrong yesterday. I hope so, anyway. I really, really hope so...

Chapter Six

"*Bon voyage*, Ellie!"

Ellie smiled at Belle and thanked her, patting her jacket pocket. "Don't worry, I've got your shopping list safe in here," she said. "Although I'm not sure I can fit half a ton of French goodies in my backpack."

"But you will try; I know you will," Belle said. "Because you are so, so kind, and such a wonderful, wonderful friend to me. . ."

"OK, OK," Ellie said, laughing at the beseeching expression in Belle's eyes. "I'll do my best." She glanced at her watch. "I'd better go. Mum should be here to pick me up any minute. We have to check in at the train station by eight-thirty."

Ellie hugged her friends goodbye and rushed downstairs to wait for her mum outside the school entrance. She was starting to feel really REALLY excited about going to Paris. She could hardly believe that, later that morning, she'd be in a whole different country, where they spoke a completely different language! Ever since she'd seen Heather, she'd been wondering what her friend was doing in France and how she was getting along with her exchange family. Ellie had also been wondering over and over again just what had gone wrong last time they'd been together. Could she have imagined Heather's coolness towards her? Had it really just been a bad case of jet lag and tiredness?

Ellie heaved her bag on to her shoulder as she saw her mum's car approaching. Hopefully she'd got it all wrong, and she and Heather were going to get along just fine. She was probably just being paranoid. Of course they'd get along and have a wonderful time in Paris together!

Ellie waved to her mum and tried to look cheerful as she opened the boot and slung her bag inside. She wouldn't dwell on it any more. She had a train to catch!

The nine-thirty train from London to Paris departed with Ellie and her mum on board. It seemed no time at all before they had reached the English coastline. There, the train left England to plunge underground into the Channel Tunnel, and under the sea to France.

Ellie was so excited that she grabbed her mum's hand and held it tightly for the twenty minutes or so until they next saw daylight. "*French* daylight!" Ellie couldn't help giggling. "Wow, Mum! We're in France now! Can you believe it? And a whole new time zone!"

Her mum gazed out of the window. "I can't, really," she admitted. "I don't think I'll really believe it until I order my first *café au lait*." She leaned back in her seat and smiled. "Isn't it wonderful, waking up in one country and having lunch in another? I can't wait to get there!"

When the long, sleek cross-channel train finally pulled into Gare du Nord, the bustling terminus in the north of Paris, Ellie was out of her seat and waiting to get off faster than you could say *croissant*. Ellie's mum had arranged to meet Heather's exchange group near the station, where they were going to join them for a bus tour of the city.

"There she is," Mrs Brown said, pointing her out to Ellie. "I'd better just say hello to the teachers, OK?"

Ellie felt a little shy as she and her mum approached the school group. She didn't recognize anybody there, except for Heather, who was listening to a girl with black plaits talking. "And he started asking me all these questions in French, and. . ."

Ellie walked up to Heather, still feeling shy. "Hi," she said.

"Hi," Heather replied. "Marcy, this is my friend, Ellie," she went on quickly as the girl with black plaits spun around to stare at the newcomer. "Ellie, this is Marcy, Nancy and Georgia. Guys, this is Ellie. Ellie and I were friends way back in fifth grade."

"Hi," Heather's friends chorused.

The girl Heather had called Marcy looked Ellie up and down briefly and then went on with the story she'd been in the middle of. "So anyway. I was like, oh help, and saying *'je ne comprends pas'* over and over, but he wasn't listening – or maybe he couldn't understand my accent, and he just kept talking in French and—"

"What à nightmare," Nancy said sympa-thetically. *"Quelle horreur!"*

"I know! But luckily Claudette came back and straightened everything out for me." Marcy rolled her eyes and Ellie was reminded of Naomi. "It's so weird, isn't it, not under-standing everything people say? Makes you feel really helpless."

"And totally dumb!" laughed Heather.

Ellie stood there, feeling slightly awkward. She'd obviously missed most of Marcy's story and didn't know who any of the people were that she was referring to. Ellie opened her mouth to ask about the French family that Heather was staying with as part of the exchange programme, but then, just at that moment, a teacher called everybody to attention. "Here's our bus. Let's get on board and go see Paris!"

A cheer went up from the students and there was a mad dash to get good seats on the bus. Ellie wasn't ready for the rush and managed to get separated from Heather and her friends. She looked around for her mum, suddenly feeling lost. Her mum was laughing and joking with the teachers. When Ellie looked over, she blew her a kiss but made no move towards her. Ellie waved a hand in reply; then she squared her shoulders. She didn't want to be the only person on the bus sitting with her *mum*, but at the same time, she felt a little unnerved as she climbed on board all alone. Where was Heather? Why hadn't she waited for Ellie?

Ellie squeezed down the aisle of the bus in-between the other students who were saving seats for one another and leaning across the aisle to chat. Right at the back of the bus were Heather and her friends, all laughing about something together and comparing cameras. Heather looked up and waved at Ellie, and a feeling of relief swept over her.

"Hi," she said, trying not to sound as shy as she felt, as she grabbed a seat in front of Heather and Marcy.

"Hi," Heather said. "I wasn't sure if you were going to be sitting with your mum or not."

"Your *mum*'s here?" Nancy asked, sounding surprised.

"Yes," Ellie said. She blushed as she saw Nancy raising her eyebrows at the other girls. "We live in England now. Mum lives in Oxford and—"

"Oh, *yeah*," Georgia said, snapping her fingers suddenly. "You're the friend Heather met up with in London!"

"Yes," said Ellie. She was somewhat surprised to realize that Heather hadn't already told them that.

"Ellie and I used to hang out all the time when we were in elementary school," Heather explained. Then she turned to Ellie. "Marcy,

Nancy and Georgia are all in my class in middle school."

"We do French together with Madame Lou-Lou," Marcy said, which made the other three burst out laughing. *"Ooh là là, mes amis!"*

"That's not her *real* name, Ell," Heather started to explain. "She—"

"Bonjour, la classe!" Marcy trilled in an exaggerated French accent. *"Comment allez-vous, mes petites?"*

Ellie started to get lost in the conversation. Although she was learning French at The Royal Ballet School, Heather and her friends seemed to be way ahead of her. She could only understand a word here and there. All of the girls were now speaking French to one another in high-pitched voices and she didn't have a clue what they were talking about. *I wish Belle were here to help me out*, Ellie thought to herself, keeping a strained smile on her face. After a while, when it became obvious that no one was going to explain what they were saying, Ellie turned around in her seat, gazing out of the bus window and tuning out of the conversation behind her.

"We are now crossing the river Seine," the tour guide said from the front of the bus. "So if you were to jump in there, you'd be truly . . . in-Seine."

A feeble laugh went around the bus. "Insane, get it?" the tour guide repeated jovially. "Now, the river Seine is. . ."

Ellie didn't laugh. Her cheeks felt hot with embarrassment. She'd come all this way to see Heather – and Heather was practically ignoring her! She tried to lose herself in the sight of the beautiful stone bridge they were travelling over instead, but couldn't help feeling left out. Heather and her friends were still giggling about their teachers and saying things in French accents to one another. *Am I ever going to have any time alone with Heather?*

Ellie wondered. At this rate, they were never going to be able to talk.

"We are now approaching one of the city's most famous landmarks, the Eiffel Tower," the tour guide said a little while later. "On a clear day, you have wonderful views over the whole of the city from the top of this magnificent tower. You could say that you get a real Eiffel. . . Eyeful, get it?"

By now everyone was ignoring the tour guide's terrible puns. All of the students craned forward, hoping for an early glimpse of the elegant iron tower.

Ellie suddenly thought of something and turned around to Heather again, peering over the back of her seat. "Hey, Heather, speaking of wonderful views, when you're back in London, I'll have to take you to the London Eye – you know, the big wheel by the River Thames?" she said. "You can see for miles from up there – all of London, it feels like."

An awkward expression passed over Heather's face. "Umm. . ." she said. "Actually . . . I've signed up for the group field trip. We're all going to go to Ham House on that Saturday – you know, that seventeenth-century royal house that's supposed to be haunted."

"Ham House," Marcy said, making grunting noises to the other girls. "*La maison de jambon!*"

Ellie was taken aback at Heather's words. "Oh," she said. "I thought we were going to meet up again."

Heather shook her head, looking rather embarrassed. "Sorry," she said. "I already paid the money to go with the others, so. . ." She shrugged. "I guess I forgot we were supposed to be meeting up."

"Oink," Marcy said conversationally. "*Je suis*. . . How do you say 'pig' in French?" She leaned across to Nancy. "Hey, Nancy, how do you say 'pig' in French?"

"Is it *cochon*?" Nancy wondered aloud. "Or *vache*?"

"*Vache* is definitely 'cow'," Georgia told them. "Don't you remember Madame Lou-Lou doing her cow impressions?"

Ellie was still gazing at Heather in disappointment. "Oh," was all she could think of to say again. "Oh. So after today. . ."

". . .we won't have a chance to see each other again before I go back to the States," Heather finished.

"I guess not," Ellie said unhappily. She felt as if she'd been slapped in the face. Her best friend from Chicago was in the same city for the first time in years — and she'd chosen to spend the time with all her school friends, instead! Talk about a snub!

"I can't wait to go ghost-hunting," Marcy was saying behind her. "What would you do if you saw a real, live ghost?"

"Don't you mean a real, *dead* ghost?" Georgia quipped.

"I think I'd scream my head off," Nancy said, giggling. "What about you, Heather?"

"Totally," Heather said, grinning. "And run a mile, too."

Ellie's cheeks flamed. Well. So that was that? Conversation over? She felt as if she'd been totally put in her place by Heather.

Ellie turned back to face the front of the bus just in time to see the Arc de Triomphe looming up before her. She felt so disappointed by what Heather had just said that she could hardly look at it. *I'm in Paris, right in front of the most beautiful Paris sights and ... I'm just not as excited as I should be*, she thought miserably. She found herself yearning suddenly for the safety and familiarity of The Royal Ballet School. *Why* didn't Heather want to see her again?

*   *   *

"I still can't believe we're here, you know," Ellie's mum said, smiling across the restaurant table at which she and Ellie were both sitting, later that day. "It seems like a dream, don't you think?"

The two of them were having dinner that evening in a small, cheerful restaurant near their hotel. But even though there were the most incredible smells of garlic and steak wafting through from the kitchen, Ellie just didn't feel hungry.

She forced a smile on to her face. "I know," she said. "It's kind of unreal, isn't it?"

"I wonder if we'll have time to go to Notre Dame in the morning before we catch our return train," her mum mused, flicking through her guidebook to show Ellie a picture of the famous old church in the centre of Paris. "It looks so beautiful. And it would be great to go right to the top of the Eiffel Tower, wouldn't it? The view must be breathtaking."

"Mmmm," Ellie said, not really listening to her mum. She was still too caught up in what had happened with Heather to think about anything else.

There was a pause, and then her mum leaned forward with a concerned look in her eyes. "Are you all right, Ellie?" she asked.

Ellie sighed and met her mum's gaze. "Kind of," she said. "Well, not really," she admitted. "Heather and I didn't get along very well. I hardly got to spend any time with her; she was with her friends the whole time. And. . ." She swallowed. This was the hardest part to say. "I don't think she likes me any more."

Ellie's mum put a hand on her arm. "Oh, honey, why do you think that?"

Ellie shrugged miserably. "She just seemed . . . cool with me. And she spent the whole day today talking to her friends, not me. I felt really left out, not knowing any of the people they were gossiping about. And they kept saying stuff in French, which I couldn't understand." She fiddled with her knife and fork, and then felt thoroughly ungrateful. Her mum had brought her all this way, to Paris, and she was moaning about it! "I mean, I'm having a good time," she backtracked hastily, "but. . ."

A waiter came over then and set down plates of steak and *frites*, hot thin chips, with bowls of salad and bread. Ellie took a hunk of crusty bread and spread butter on to it. "She was kind of offhand with me after we spent the day in London together, too," she confessed. "Did you notice how quiet she was? I thought it was just jet lag, but now I think maybe she just didn't want to spend time with me after all."

Ellie's mum thought for a moment. "I'm sure she *did* want to spend time with you," she said after a while. "When she e-mailed me from

Chicago to arrange it, she sounded really excited about seeing you again." She hesitated for a moment, and then went on. "Ellie, do you remember how you felt things had changed when you came back to Oxford after being at The Royal Ballet School for half a term?" she asked. "Suddenly Phoebe had all these new friends and you felt left out?"

Ellie nodded. Of course she remembered! She'd felt really upset at the time. It had been awful, truly awful, when she and Phoebe had arranged to meet up after not seeing each other for so long, and Phoebe had turned up with all her new friends in tow – new friends that Ellie didn't know.

"Well," her mum went on. "Do you think maybe Heather felt the same way you did then, when she came to London?"

Ellie's knife almost fell out of her fingers as the realization struck her. How could she not have seen it earlier?

"I brought all my school friends along to the West End, when it was supposed to be just me and Heather," she said slowly, feeling aghast at her own insensitivity. "And with one thing and another, I didn't manage to give her very much time." She groaned. "And all that ballet talk! Heather must have felt as left out as I did today!"

Ellie's mum's eyes were sympathetic. "I think so," she agreed.

Ellie put her head in her hands. "No wonder Heather has been cool with me," she said. "I did to her what Phoebe did to me. And now I won't get to see her again to apologize before she goes back to Chicago!"

Dear Diary,
I feel like such a jerk — I've gone and ruined everything with Heather now. How could I have been so stupid? As soon as Mum reminded me about what had happened with Phoebe last

year, I could have kicked myself.

That's totally why Heather seemed so unfriendly when we said goodbye in London. She must have been mad that I had dragged so many other friends out on our special day together. And I can't even e-mail her or call her to say sorry, now that I've figured out what was wrong.

I've blown it, haven't I? I've truly blown it.

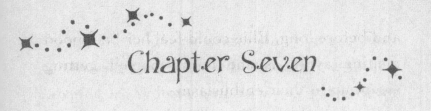
Ellie was downcast when she returned to school the following day. Everyone expected her to have had a wonderful time in Paris, and she found it difficult to be very enthusiastic about her day there. She felt so despondent about what had happened with Heather that she changed the subject whenever anybody asked her what she'd been doing. She didn't even feel like telling Grace about it yet. *I must be the most ungrateful person in the world*, she thought dolefully. *Who else would go to Paris and come back with a face as long as mine?*

Luckily, her friends were starting to get seriously excited about the forthcoming visit of Lim Soo May and Christopher Blackwell, and before long, Ellie could feel her bad mood melting away as she found herself getting swept up in their enthusiasm.

Grace had been home for the weekend and had brought back with her some of her own ballet videos, which starred the famous couple. The Year 7 and 8 girls' common room was packed on Sunday evening as everyone settled down to watch the stars performing.

"Oh, I love this one!" Belle sighed happily as *Sleeping Beauty* began. She tucked her legs underneath her and leaned back against a cushion. "It is even better, I think, that they are in love in real life. You can see it when they dance, *non*?"

"I read somewhere that they actually fell in love during rehearsals for *Sleeping Beauty*," Lara chimed in, her eyes glued to the set. "How romantic can you get?"

"It was *Swan Lake*, not *Sleeping Beauty*," Kate put in. She was sitting at the table in the far corner of the room playing a computer game.

"Was it? Are you sure?" Lara asked.

Kate blinked at the question and two pink spots appeared on her cheeks. "I think I saw it in a magazine or something," she replied, still staring at the computer screen.

Lara shrugged. "Well, it's still romantic to fall in love with your leading man, whatever the ballet, isn't it?" she said.

"Somebody's been doing their homework on the celebs," Naomi said teasingly, turning to look at Kate with interest. "Although I thought *you* weren't *interested* in celebrities, Kate?"

Ellie noticed that Kate's shoulders stiffened ever so slightly at the question.

"I'm not," Kate said shortly, still playing her game.

"I saw this thing on the Internet that said Lim Soo May almost didn't train as a ballerina at all," Grace said chattily. "She was really good at gymnastics, too, and had to decide between the two." She watched as the dancer did a series of *pirouettes* across the screen, and sighed in admiration. "I am so glad she chose to come to The Royal Ballet School."

"I can't believe they're going to be here on Tuesday," Naomi said excitedly, bouncing on the sofa in time to the music. "Just *hours* to go, people! Hours!"

Ellie could feel her spirits lifting at the thought. "Come on!" she cried suddenly, leaping off her chair. "I'm going to get in some extra practice. Anybody going to come and be Sleeping Beauty with me?"

"Dancing Beauty, I think you mean," Grace chuckled, unfolding her long legs from the sofa and following Ellie to the door. "Definitely."

"Me too, I think," Belle decided. "We can watch videos any time. But I need to practise straight away!"

The next morning in their regular ballet class, Ellie worked even harder than she usually did. She was determined to polish up every single aspect of her ballet as best as she could before she had to dance in front of prima ballerina Lim Soo May tomorrow. She wasn't the only one.

"Goodness, what devoted students I have today," Ms Wells said after they'd warmed up at the barre. "Anyone would think something special was happening tomorrow!" she teased.

"What time will they be here, Ms Wells?" Ellie couldn't help asking.

"The film crew will arrive first thing," her teacher replied. "They're going to film Soo May and Christopher arriving, and then meeting their old teachers, and so on."

As Ms Wells paused for breath, Ellie realized that every girl was hanging on their teacher's words.

"We will start our class as usual, although we'll be in the Fonteyn Studio rather than here," Ms Wells continued. "Year 7 girls will have class in MF1 and Year 7 boys in MF2." The large Margot Fonteyn Studio could be divided by a floor-to-ceiling partition to create two studios when necessary. "Sometime during class, Ms Bell and Anna Masters will bring Soo May and Christopher in to join us. Everyone knows Anna, don't they?"

Ellie nodded along with the others. Of course everybody knew Anna Masters! She worked in The Royal Ballet Upper School building in Covent Garden as the school's marketing and public relations director, but she frequently visited White Lodge too, arranging media visits or press conferences. She was going to be overseeing the production of this programme, by the sound of it.

"Soo May and Christopher will observe the rest of your class and the boys', and then there'll be a bit of time to talk with them afterwards. Does that sound OK with everybody?" Ms Wells smiled as she asked the question; it was obvious she knew what the answer was going to be.

The studio rang with a resounding "Yes!" in reply.

"Good," Ms Wells said, her eyes twinkling. "Now, I expect you'd like to practise your *port de bras*," she went on. "Nobody wants to get their arms in a tangle in front of Lim Soo May, do they?"

The atmosphere was one of feverish concentration as Ellie and the rest of the girls worked on their *port de bras* and then moved on to work in the centre of the studio.

Ellie was concentrating so hard that Kate's voice seemed to come out of nowhere when she spoke.

"Ms Wells? Please may I go? I don't feel very well."

Ellie turned her head to see her friend clutching a hand to her stomach.

"What's wrong, Kate?" Ms Wells asked, motioning for the pianist to stop playing.

"I just feel a bit faint – and sick," Kate said in a weak-sounding voice. "I think I need to lie down."

"Oh dear, I hope you're not coming down with anything," Ms Wells said in concern. "Maybe you should go and see the school nurse." She glanced around, and her eyes fell upon Ellie. "Ellie, would you mind taking Kate to the school nurse?"

"Of course not," Ellie said, running to grab her sweatpants at once. Poor Kate! "Come on," she said, putting an arm around her friend and shepherding her towards the door. "I hope you're going to be better for tomorrow."

"I'm not sure I will be," Kate said dolefully, picking up her ballet bag. "I feel terrible, like I'm coming down with a bug or something."

"Oh, no!" Ellie cried. "You can't – you just can't be! Oh, I hope the nurse can help you out, Kate."

Once Ellie and Kate had reached the health centre, Ellie promised to come back and see her after ballet class, and then ran back to the studio. She felt so sorry for Kate. What a time to come down with something!

When ballet class had ended, Ellie and Naomi went to the health centre to see how Kate was feeling before they showered and changed for their maths class.

Kate was lying in bed with her eyes shut.

"I've looked her over," the nurse told Ellie and Naomi in a low voice, "but I can't see anything wrong with her. Has she been overdoing things lately, working too hard?"

Ellie and Naomi looked at each other. "No more than usual, I'd say," Ellie said. In fact, Kate was about the only girl in Year 7 who *hadn't* been cramming in extra practice at all hours of the day.

"Do you think she'll be OK for tomorrow?" Naomi asked.

The nurse glanced over at Kate again. "I don't see why not. She'll just have to take things easy today, get lots of rest."

"Tell her we stopped by, won't you?" Naomi asked. "We'd better go and get changed now, Ellie. I don't think Mr Best would be too pleased if we arrived at his maths class in our leotards."

"Thanks," Ellie said to the nurse. "We'll come back later on."

Naomi whistled as they ran to their dorm. "What a nightmare," she said sympathetically. "It's such bad luck for Kate. Imagine getting ill right before one of the most exciting days at The Royal Ballet School so far!" She shook her head. "And Kate would have really had a shot at being picked for Lim Soo May's class, too. She is such a fantastic dancer."

"I know," Ellie agreed. "I was thinking that Kate, Belle and Lara would get picked. Or maybe Grace. Or. . ."

"Or maybe you, Ellie Brown," Naomi said, elbowing her as they hurried into the dorm.

Ellie pulled a face. "In my dreams," she said, peeling off her sweaty leotard and kicking off her ballet shoes.

"Don't write yourself off," Naomi said, sounding more serious than usual. "I was watching you today – you looked really good. Easily good enough to be picked."

Ellie smiled. "Well, you never know," she joked, grabbing her towel and heading for the showers. "If Belle and Lara come down with Kate's mystery illness too, I might have a shot!"

Ellie knew she was being deliberately flippant about her chances of being chosen for the masterclass. She felt as though she couldn't dare let herself hope she might be picked. She wanted it so badly! *Well*, she thought to herself, shampooing her hair quickly, *this time tomorrow, the class will be over. And then we'll know who the lucky ones are!*

After tuck that afternoon, Ellie popped into the health centre once more to see how Kate was doing. "Hello," she said, putting her head around the door. "Anybody—?"

Ellie stopped. Kate's bed was empty – and Kate was racing to get her ringing mobile from her bag at the other end of the sick room!

"Oh!" Ellie exclaimed. "Hi, Kate." Kate certainly didn't look ill any more – but her face was a picture of guilt. What was going on?

Kate glanced at the caller display on her phone and let the call go to voicemail. "Um. . . Hi, Ellie," she said.

Ellie frowned, feeling a little confused. Was

Kate sick or not? "So, you're feeling better?" Ellie asked.

Kate shifted her feet around and looked down at the floor.

"Um . . . yes," she said. "A little sleep sorted me out. It must have been one of those bugs that you get over really quickly. . ." Her voice trailed away uncertainly.

"Great!" Ellie said, but she couldn't help feeling curious. Something fishy was definitely going on. Why was Kate still in the sick room if she was well enough to race across the room to get her phone? And who had the call been from? Was it her secret boyfriend on the line again? "Hey, now you'll be able to see Lim Soo May and Christopher Blackwell tomorrow," she went on brightly. "That's good news."

Kate shrugged. "I guess so," she said, not looking Ellie in the eye.

Ellie couldn't bear it any more. "Kate —

what's wrong?" she asked. "What's going on? You've been acting so strangely lately, and. . ."

Kate shook her head. "Nothing's wrong," she said cagily. There was a pause.

Ellie took a deep breath. She was determined to confront all this secrecy now – it had gone on for far too long. "Kate, I know this might sound a little crazy," Ellie went on, "but . . . were you really sick? Or is something else going on?"

Kate walked quickly across the room to Ellie and lowered her voice. "OK, to tell the truth, I wasn't sick," she said.

"So why did you pretend you were?" Ellie asked, struggling to understand. "I don't get it, Kate."

Kate bit her lip, looking anguished at the question. "I just. . ." There was a long pause and then Kate finally looked Ellie in the face. "I can't say," she replied eventually. "It's really complicated." Her eyes were beseeching. "Ellie, will you please keep this to yourself, and not tell the others?" she asked. "I'm sorry I can't tell you what's going on. That's just how it is. Anyway, it's nothing much. Really. I just. . ."

She shrugged and Ellie wasn't fooled for an instant. *Nothing much? Yeah, right!*

"Please?" Kate repeated.

Ellie looked at her friend, feeling concerned. "If it's such a big deal to you, then—"

"It is," Kate said quickly, before Ellie could finish.

"Then, sure, I'll keep it to myself," Ellie replied, not knowing what else to say. "I won't ask you anything else, if you don't want to talk about . . . whatever's going on."

"I don't," Kate mumbled. "Thanks, Ellie."

"OK," Ellie said, none the wiser. "So. . . Are you going to character class? It's starting in a few minutes."

Kate put her mobile in her pocket and sighed. "I suppose so," she said.

The nurse bustled in at that moment – and smiled when she saw Kate out of bed and standing talking to Ellie. "Ah, good! There's more colour in your cheeks now," she said. "Feeling better?"

Kate blushed. "Yes," she replied, not looking at Ellie. "I think I just needed a sleep," she said lamely.

The nurse gave Kate a curious look. "Too much chatting after lights out, eh?" she asked. "Honestly! You girls! Straight to sleep tonight, OK?"

Kate nodded, her eyes downcast as she picked up her school bag.

Dear Diary,

I knew something was going on with Kate – and that's definite now. But what? And why is she becoming so distant from all of her friends? I'm so surprised she deliberately faked being sick. What was all that about? That's not like her!

Great news from home tonight, though. Mum's come to the rescue again! She suggested that we both go to Ham House the same day as Heather's trip in the hope of seeing her there. It's my last chance to make things OK again between us — so of course I said yes! I just hope I can save our friendship before Heather flies back to Chicago...

Chapter Eight

As soon as Ellie's eyes opened the next morning, her instincts reminded her that there was something really exciting happening that day. A broad smile spread across her face. "Hey, Grace!" she hissed, sitting up in bed and leaning towards Grace on her left. "Our special visitors are arriving today – wake up!"

Grace's eyes opened wide at Ellie's words. "I've dreamed about it all night," she said, stretching her arms above her head. She yawned and stuck her toes out the end of her bed. "In my dream, though, I was right in the middle of the observed class and I looked down to see I'd forgotten to put my leotard on – I was dancing in nothing but a pair of ballet shoes!"

Ellie chuckled softly, pulling on her bathrobe. "Don't worry, Grace, I won't let you go in there in your birthday suit," she said. Then she raised her voice, unable to resist waking her other friends on such a momentous day. "Hey, guys," she called. "Guys! Lim Soo May's here!"

Every single girl in the dorm who wasn't already awake lifted her head from the pillow with a start.

"What? Where?" Lara cried, rubbing the sleep from her eyes.

Naomi, who was definitely not a morning person, groaned as she realized she'd been tricked, and threw a hairbrush at Ellie. "Ellie Brown! I was having such a nice dream, then," she said. Then she sat up, looking wide awake. "Oh, it's today!" she remembered aloud, and all of a sudden, she stopped looking so bad-tempered. "Oh, that's OK. I don't mind you waking me up at all, if it's today!"

"You are being very confusing, Naomi," Belle commented, chuckling. "But I think I know what you are saying. I am glad to be awake too. It's OK to be woken up for such an exciting day, yes?"

The dorm was soon buzzing with laughter and voices, as everybody discussed the day ahead.

"I don't know if I'll be able to manage any breakfast; I'm so excited!" Naomi said.

"That'll be a first then," quipped Bryony.

The only person who wasn't giggling and smiling was Kate.

"Everything all right?" Ellie asked in a low voice, as she found herself next to Kate in the shared bathroom.

Kate was brushing her teeth at the long row of sinks, and frowning into the mirror. *She looks as if she hardly slept*, Ellie thought, squeezing toothpaste on to her own toothbrush.

Kate nodded and busied herself rinsing with mouthwash, before turning to Ellie. "Fine," she said breezily, grabbing her shower bag and returning to the dorm.

Ellie gazed after her while she brushed her teeth. Kate was definitely *not* fine, that was pretty obvious. Ellie sighed, remembering their conversation in the health centre. Well, Kate sure wasn't going to say anything other than "fine" right now, she knew that much. She grimaced at her own reflection. Hopefully, the world-famous dancers would bring a smile to Kate's face. If meeting Lim Soo May didn't cheer a Royal Ballet School student up, Ellie didn't know what would!

After breakfast, Ellie and the others made their way back towards the dorm to prepare for ballet class. As they entered the lobby, four people were setting up film equipment. They all watched as one man adjusted a large camera he rested over one shoulder, while a woman wearing an earpiece gave him directions about where to stand. Another woman was setting up a couple of lights while another man adjusted a huge boom microphone.

Anna Masters was standing by, answering the crew's questions and offering advice. "Hi, girls!" she called cheerily as she caught sight of Ellie and the others. "All ready for this morning's visitors?"

They all smiled and nodded, and then made their way up the staircase.

"Oh, dear — I'm so nervous, I feel sick!" Grace hissed to Ellie.

"You're not the only one!" said Megan, overhearing.

In fact, as Ellie and her friends changed into their ballet clothes and prepared for their class, everybody seemed jittery with nerves.

"I can't believe I'm having a bad hair day

today," wailed Naomi as her bun came loose for the third time. "Typical!"

"Naomi, Lim Soo May is going to judge you on your dancing, not your hair," Ellie pointed out, giving her own hair an extra blast of hairspray, just to be on the safe side.

"She won't be able to take her eyes *off* my hair if it keeps flapping about all over the place," Naomi grumbled, trying to tuck the loose strands in. "Right – that's it. I'm cutting it all off. Who's got some scissors?"

"Come here," Grace said, taking her comb over to Naomi. "No baldies in class today, Ms Crawford. Let me sort you out."

"Has anybody seen my hairnet?" Lara fretted.

"Do I look OK?" Belle wanted to know.

"Can I borrow somebody's hairspray?" Bryony cried, tossing her empty can into the bin with a clang.

"Does my leotard look too wrinkly?" Ellie

asked, trying to smooth it out with her fingers. *Oh why didn't I hang it up neatly yesterday?* she thought.

"I don't want to alarm anybody. . ." Megan called from the far end of the dorm. "But we've only got two minutes before we're expected in class."

"HELP!" cried the whole of the dorm as one.

Ellie gave her leotard a last frantic smoothing before flinging it on, with her sweatsuit on top. Now that she thought about it, a wrinkled leotard was the least of her worries. How was she ever going to be able to *dance* today, she wondered, when her legs felt so wobbly?

A minute or so later, Ellie and the rest of the Year 7 girls had rushed out of the dorm and were jostling their way back to the staircase.

As her foot hit the top step, Ellie saw that

the film crew was now poised at the open entrance, ready for action. Anna Masters and Miss Purvis, the head of the Lower School, were waiting next to them. Ellie immediately stopped in her tracks, as did the others.

"Wow," Naomi breathed, her eyes glued to the scene. "Soo May and Christopher must be about to appear!"

As if she'd heard Naomi's words, the woman wearing the earpiece suddenly motioned to the cameraman. "Here we go!" she called. And then, seeing the girls all watching on the stairs, added, "Everybody quiet, please! Filming in five . . . four . . . three . . . two . . . one!" She mouthed the last two numbers, holding up two fingers, then one, and then stepped nimbly out of the way of the camera. Ellie realized she must be the director of the film. A deathly hush spread over the girls.

Right on cue, in came none other than Lim

Soo May and Christopher Blackwell. Miss Purvis stepped forward to greet them, her movement followed by the cameraman.

"Soo May, Christopher, welcome back to The Royal Ballet School," Miss Purvis began. "We are all so thrilled to see you here again."

The dancers were smiling and looking around. "It's wonderful to be back," Soo May said in a clear, sweet voice.

"It seems only yesterday I was running through this foyer, late for one of my ballet classes," Christopher added.

"And . . . cut!" the director called. "Lovely – but can we just check your mike, Soo May? We're picking up some background noise."

As the sound technician ran over to Soo May, Anna Masters gazed up and saw Ellie and her friends on the stairs. "Sorry to keep you girls," she called. "You can come on through now. We don't want you to be late for your class."

Ellie felt ridiculously self-conscious as she and the other Year 7 girls continued their way down the stairs in order to skirt around the film crew and dancers. She desperately wanted to stare long and hard at the famous stars – but felt too embarrassed at the thought of being caught gawking.

"Um . . . I've just forgotten something," Kate muttered suddenly, as they neared the bottom of the steps. Without another word, she turned and ran back to the dorm, her cheeks bright pink.

"I knew it," Lara hissed to Ellie. "Look over there – William Forrest! It is William she's been seeing on the sly. He must be her secret boyfriend!"

Ellie glanced across the lobby to where William was coming in from the other direction. "Do you think so?" she asked.

"I know so," Lara said confidently. "Why else would Kate charge off like that? She's avoiding him now, isn't she? That must be what this is all about!"

"Did you see how pink her cheeks were?" Naomi added, eavesdropping. She smirked and nodded. "Busted, Kate Walker. Totally busted!"

"This way, Ellie," Grace said, grabbing her by the arm and steering her along as they walked around the film crew and the star visitors. "Are you spacing out?"

Ellie laughed at herself. She'd been thinking so hard about Kate and William that she was heading to their normal ballet studio on automatic pilot. She'd totally forgotten that they were going to dance in the Margot Fonteyn Studio today, rather than in their usual studio.

Ellie suddenly felt shivery with nerves as they filed into MF1. The last time she'd danced in the Margot Fonteyn Studio had been for her Year 7 appraisal, back in February. The thought that she'd been dancing to ensure her future at the school had been really scary. And now, here she was again, with the prospect of dancing in front of two international superstars!

As Ellie stripped off her sweatsuit and went to the barre for the first warm-up stretches, all thoughts of Kate vanished. Time to concentrate on her ballet now. There was no room in her head for anything else.

The lesson began as normal, but when the door opened a couple of minutes later, everyone stopped their *pliés* to look. Kate crept in, scarlet-faced, and there was an almost audible sigh of disappointment when they saw that it wasn't the two stars.

"Come on, girls," Ms Wells said to them. "I know you're excited about this morning, but try to treat this as an everyday thing. If you get too wound up, you won't be able to dance your best for Soo May."

Ellie returned to her *pliés*, trying to block everything out of her head other than the slow stretching of her legs, the position of her feet and her head, and the sensation of her muscles lengthening, as her body sank into the movement. *Do this right*, she urged herself. *If you're not warmed up properly, you'll pull a muscle in front of Lim Soo May, and that would be disastrous!*

Despite her best intentions, when the door opened an hour or so later during the *adage* section of class, Ellie's head spun around to see who had come in. So did everyone else's.

This time there was an excited-sounding intake of breath as every student in the room watched Ms Bell, the Lower School Ballet Principal, lead Soo May and Christopher into the studio, followed by Anna Masters and the film crew.

"Hello, everybody," Ms Bell said. "I'm sure

our special guests need no introduction, and you all know why we are here today: to select students to take part in a masterclass with Soo May and Christopher. We are going to be watching part of your class this morning. Lim Soo May will be concentrating on the girls, while Christopher observes the boys."

"I hope nobody minds too much," said Christopher with a winning smile.

"Hi, girls. I'll be very quiet; I promise," Soo May added. "Just forget all about me watching you."

Ellie smiled. Like that could ever happen!

Soo May looked around the studio and gave a little laugh. "You know, this studio used to seem frighteningly enormous to me when I was a Year 7 like you," she said confidingly.

Dressed in a pale blue hooded top and fashionable jeans, with her glossy black hair tied back in a simple ponytail, Lim Soo May seemed so . . . normal! Still, even in casual clothes, she looked every part a ballerina, with her graceful neck, delicate features, and the elegant way she carried herself. It blew Ellie away that Lim Soo May had really been a schoolgirl here at The Royal Ballet School, just like herself.

"I'm going to take Christopher to the Year 7 boys' class in MF2 now, and then I'll come straight back to MF1 to oversee the filming," Anna Masters explained to the class.

Christopher followed her out. He turned to give the class a wave, mouthing, "Good luck, everyone!"

"Soo May, would you like to sit here?" Ms Bell asked, pulling chairs for them both at the front of the studio.

As Soo May and Ms Bell were getting settled, Ellie felt Naomi elbowing her in the ribs and suddenly had to fight the urge to giggle. She was so nervous – yet so excited!

A couple of minutes later Anna Masters

returned. It was time to carry on with the class.

Kate raised her hand. "Ms Wells, my mouth has suddenly gone all dry – please may I go to the water fountain?" she asked. Her cheeks were pink, and Ellie guessed she was a little embarrassed to be asking such a question in front of a superstar.

Then Grace put *her* hand up. "Um. . . Can I go, too?" she mumbled.

Ms Wells nodded. "Of course. Anyone else been hit by an attack of nerves?"

Soo May was still smiling as Kate and Grace scuttled out of the studio. "Please! There really is no need to be nervous. It's not so long ago that I was studying here myself. I'm just going to watch you, that's all."

Lim Soo May had such a natural, relaxed manner about her that Ellie was already starting to feel more comfortable being in the same room as her.

Once the film crew was happy that everything was ready, and Kate and Grace were back in their places in the centre of the studio, the lesson continued.

Ellie was absolutely determined not to wobble in front of Lim Soo May and Ms Bell. Out of the corner of her eye she saw them watching the class intently and discussing the students.

"That's it, Naomi – slowly does it," Ms Wells's voice rang out. "And one and TWO, and one and TWO – Kate, keep to the rhythm, please."

Ellie was surprised to find how quickly she settled down under the eye of the famous ballerina. Her nerves were completely gone, she realized with a start, as Ms Wells talked them through a sequence that she wanted them to follow. *Pas de chat, pas de chat*, then a *chassé* into an *arabesque*, and on it went.

The pianist began to play a bouncy, staccato

piece of music and the class danced together. Kate was dancing in front of Ellie and Ellie was surprised to see what a hash she was making of it. Kate did the *chassé* the wrong way, then performed the wobbliest *arabesque* Ellie had ever seen. Ellie tried to stop staring and concentrate on her own steps. She couldn't help being taken aback, though. It wasn't like Kate at all to dance like this; in fact, Ellie couldn't ever remember seeing her friend dance quite as badly before. If she hadn't known better, she'd have thought Kate was still feeling ill from the day before. It was as if she'd completely fallen apart under the pressure.

Ms Wells had them practise the sequence several times through and soon all the girls had the steps down pat – all except for Kate. It was as if she couldn't remember a thing Ms Wells was saying, getting the steps in the wrong order every time.

Ms Wells motioned to the pianist to stop, then, with a sympathetic gaze at Kate, asked the girls to line up at one side of the studio to perform a series of *pirouettes*.

Ellie could see Lim Soo May talking with a serious expression to Ms Bell and shaking her head a little. She hoped for Kate's sake that they weren't ruling her friend out just yet. Kate was such a good dancer – Ellie hoped she could get over her attack of nerves, and go on to dazzle the celebrity visitor with her usual skill.

Kate was near the front of the line. With her eyes cast down to the floor, she didn't seem to be enjoying herself one bit. Ellie knew the feeling. She herself had almost blown her Final Audition for The Royal Ballet School with a mistake, and had found it very difficult to keep dancing afterwards, when all she could feel was misery, convinced that she'd wrecked everything. No doubt Kate was feeling similarly down on herself after her poor performance just now.

Grace, too, looked pale, and kept glancing up at the cameras. Grace always got nervous when it came to performing under pressure, but Kate was usually cool as a cucumber. *Perhaps she was seriously camera-shy*, Ellie thought. Or still rattled from seeing William earlier? Or maybe she'd heard the comments Lara and Naomi had made about Kate having a secret boyfriend!

Ellie forced herself to stop thinking about Kate and watch the *pirouettes*. Lara was going first. Ellie watched Lara waiting for her cue, looking confident and relaxed. Then the music started, and away she went.

Lara spun across the floor lightly, with clean precise movements, back straight, head held perfectly. The sun poured through the large high studio windows, lighting up Lara's red hair with a fiery glow. *Wonderful*, Ellie thought to herself, watching her friend smile with pleasure as she reached the other side. *No sign of stage fright there!*

Naomi did *pirouettes* across next – with a few wobbles, but a big smile on her face the whole time. Ellie found herself smiling too. Even though her technique wasn't flawless, Naomi just loved to perform!

Kate was up next. Her eyes were still down on the floor as she shuffled to the starting spot.

"Head up, Kate," Ms Wells reminded her. "And when you're ready. . . Off you go."

Kate set off rather clumsily, a strange, stiff expression on her face. Around she went once, twice . . . and then she was so off balance, she fell to the floor, landing awkwardly. "Ow!" she cried. "My ankle!"

"Oh, my goodness – darling!" came another voice. "Are you OK?"

To the surprise of every other girl in the studio, Lim Soo May rushed over to Kate –

and put her arms around her! "Oh, sweetheart," she cried in concern. "Try to keep still." Pale-faced, she turned and called over to Anna Masters. "Could you fetch Chris please, Anna? Tell him Kate has hurt herself!"

Anna Masters hurried over to the door, turning back to the film crew as she did so. "Would you stop filming, please?" she said. "Lim Soo May won't want this in the documentary. Her daughter is keen to avoid any type of singling out."

Ellie and her friends stared at one another, open-mouthed. *Her daughter?* Kate was Lim Soo May's *daughter?*

Seconds later, Christopher Blackwell rushed in, looking alarmed. "What happened? Oh, Kate!" he cried, running over to her.

Kate had tears in her eyes. "It was my own stupid fault, Chris," she confessed dolefully. "I was trying to dance badly on purpose and my ankle just gave way. . ."

Shaking his head, Christopher carefully picked Kate up from the studio floor. "Sweetheart! Why on earth—"

Ms Bell gently interrupted. "First things first, let's get that ankle seen to," she said. "I'll come with you to the nurse, Chris. This way. . ."

And then they were gone, with Soo May rushing after them.

There was a stunned silence. Ellie was still open-mouthed, trying to piece everything together. So Lim Soo May was Kate's *mother*! She hadn't seen that one coming. No *wonder* why Kate had been acting so weirdly lately! Secret boyfriend? More like secret parents! But why was she so terrified about her secret getting out? Ellie would have been proud about having such talented parents. She'd never have hidden the fact from anybody!

The other girls were looking as flabbergasted

as Ellie. "Did that really just happen?" Lara asked faintly, staring at the studio door that was still swinging.

"Yes," Ms Wells said. "It did. Lim Soo May is Kate's mother – and Christopher Blackwell is her stepfather."

"But Kate's surname is *Walker*," Naomi said, frowning.

Ms Wells nodded. "Kate's father's surname is Walker," she explained. "But he and Soo May separated when Kate was quite young. She married Christopher a couple of years ago." She paused and a serious look came over her face. "I am only telling you this now that you know the truth about Kate – but for Kate's sake, please keep it to yourselves unless she tells you otherwise."

"But ... but ... Kate lives with her grandmother in Newcastle," Ellie said. Kate had never spoken about her parents before. Knowing that Kate was half-Korean, Ellie had somehow assumed that her mum still lived in Korea.

"Yes," Ms Wells replied. "She does live with her grandmother – while Soo May and Christopher travel around the world on various ballet tours. They didn't want her education to become disrupted."

There was a silence as everybody digested the information. Ellie still couldn't believe it. And to think they'd all guessed Kate was getting twitchy because she was having a secret romance with William Forrest!

Anna Masters came over to Ms Wells. "Is it OK with you if we continue with the class so that the crew can get the shots they need, Ms Wells?" she asked.

Ms Wells suddenly looked over at the film crew as if she'd forgotten they were there. "Oh, of course, Anna," she said.

"Great, thanks." Anna smiled. She turned to the crew. "We can pass the footage to Soo

May and Christopher for them to look at later," she called.

Ms Wells called for Bryony, the next girl in line, to perform her *pirouettes* as if nothing had happened, but the girls could barely concentrate.

"I can't *believe* it," Grace whispered to Ellie. "I just can't believe it!"

"Me neither," Ellie whispered back, shaking her head. Their friend Kate, the daughter of a world-class ballerina! Who would have thought?!

Chapter Nine

As soon as ballet class was over, Ellie pulled on her sweatsuit as fast as she could and then she, Naomi and Grace rushed to the health centre to find out what had happened to Kate. The three of them dashed through the door and scanned the sick room, which was empty.

"Can I help you, girls?" the nurse asked.

"Is Kate here?" Naomi asked.

The nurse was filling in some paperwork. "She's gone to hospital for an X-ray," she replied.

"An X-ray? She hasn't *broken* her ankle, has she?" Grace asked, looking aghast at the thought. They all knew how serious a broken ankle could be to a dancer's career.

The nurse gave the girls a kind smile. "We hope it's just a sprain, but they want to check it out, just to be sure," she told them. "Mrs Hall's with her, and her mum, so she's being looked after. I'm sure Mrs Hall will call in as soon as there's any news."

"Thanks," Ellie said, and they turned to go back to the dorm, to shower. "Oh, poor Kate," she said, with feeling.

"Poor Kate? Do you really think so?" Naomi had a shrewd look in her eyes. "You heard what she said, she was dancing badly on purpose!"

"But why?" Ellie asked. "Why would she do that? We all know Kate's one of the best."

"She is. *We* know that. And I'm sure her parents know that, too," Naomi replied. "But I've been trying to work out what's been going on in Kate's head, and—"

"Please enlighten us!" Grace interrupted. "I've got absolutely no idea. I just don't get why she didn't tell us that she had such a famous mum in the first place."

"Don't you?" Naomi asked. "Imagine . . . coming to The Royal Ballet School and everybody knowing that you're Lim Soo May's daughter. Talk about pressure to prove yourself! And all those people whispering behind your back about, 'Oh, she only got in because of her mum,' that kind of thing. And gossips like us, asking her loads of questions about her parents. . ."

"What, *us*, gossip?" Ellie asked, rolling her eyes.

Grace was nodding, her eyes thoughtful. "You're right. I never thought about it like that," she said. "People would always be saying, 'Ooh, not quite as good as her mum,' or 'Oh, when Soo May was your age, Kate, she was doing blah, blah, blah. . .'"

"She'd be totally in her mum's shadow," Ellie agreed, starting to imagine how hard it would have been for Kate if everybody had known the truth, right from the start. "She'd never be allowed to stand on her own."

"And she might have got away with keeping it secret, too, if this documentary hadn't been dreamed up," Naomi mused. She snapped her fingers suddenly, realizing something. "So that phone call when she sounded so upset. . ."

". . .must have been to her mum," Ellie said, working it out at the same time. "The flowers must have come from her, too."

"And the reason she wasn't dancing well today was because she didn't want to get picked for the masterclass," Grace said as they pushed open the dormitory door. "Oh, poor Kate! She must have thought we'd all be muttering about favouritism if we'd found out."

"Like we would do such a thing!" Ellie cried indignantly.

"What a mess!" Naomi said.

Lara, Belle and Bryony looked up expectantly as the girls came in. "What's the news?" Lara asked at once. "How's Kate?"

Ellie quickly filled them in on what the nurse had told them, and what she, Naomi and Grace had just worked out. She'd realized, too, that Kate must have faked her sickness yesterday in order to get out of being in the observed class all together – only, true to her promise, she didn't tell the other girls this.

"I can't believe Kate risked getting herself injured today just to avoid being picked for the masterclass." Lara whistled. "She really didn't want anybody to make the connection, did she?"

"And now she might have a broken ankle!" Belle said, shaking her head. "That is *terrible, ça!*"

"I wish she would have trusted us with the

truth," Bryony said, looking sad. "We wouldn't have judged her."

Naomi shrugged. "No, *we* wouldn't — but there's bound to be somebody who would have, somewhere along the line," she said. "Even if nobody said anything to her face, you can bet a creep like Oliver Stafford would have made a few comments about it."

"Yeah, and maybe she didn't want complete strangers staring at her in the corridors," Grace added. "Or whispering about her, or pestering her for autographs, or. . ." She didn't need to go on. Everybody was nodding.

"It must have been awful, having to keep a secret like that all to herself," Ellie said. "But now that we know the truth, we just have to show her that it doesn't make any difference to us."

"Of course it doesn't," Lara agreed at once.

"No way," Naomi added. There was a slight pause. "Although I might just have to do the pestering-for-autographs thing," she confessed sheepishly. "Do you think she'd mind?"

"Kate!"

"You're back! Is everything all right?"

"What did the doctors say?"

As soon as Kate appeared later that afternoon, she was mobbed with hugs by Ellie and the rest of the Year 7 girls. They were in the canteen having their afternoon tuck when she limped in, leaning on a crutch, with one foot wrapped up. Lim Soo May was hovering at her side, looking anxious, and Christopher Blackwell was close behind, too. At once, all drinks and snacks were forgotten as Kate's friends rushed over to see her.

"Your ankle!" Ellie said, gulping at the sight of the bandage. "It's not broken, is it?"

Kate shook her head. "Just a sprain," she told them. "I twisted it when I fell." She seemed rather agitated, Ellie noticed, and not able to meet any of them in the eye.

"She should be dancing again in just a few weeks," Lim Soo May told them, putting a protective hand on Kate's shoulder. "The doctors think it will be fine by then."

"Oh, phew," Naomi said, and hugged Kate. "You silly girl," she scolded. "Did you really dance those *pirouettes* badly on purpose?"

Kate looked shamefaced. "Yes," she admitted. She sighed. "I suppose you all know the reason why now, too."

"I *thought* something strange was going on," Lim Soo May said, a worried frown appearing on her face. "I know you can dance far, far better than that. But why would you do such a thing, Kate?"

Kate hung her head. "Because I didn't want to get picked for your masterclass," she said heavily. "But I couldn't think of any other way out of it." She looked up at her friends and took a deep breath. "I'm sorry I've been deceiving you," she said. "I probably should have told you the truth about my parents right from the start but. . ."

"The truth about us?" Christopher asked, leaning forward. "What do you mean, Kate?"

There was a pause. Kate bit her lip. "I haven't told anybody here about you and Mum," she confessed. "I mean – the teachers know, obviously. But I begged them to keep it a secret because. . ."

"Because what?" Lim Soo May asked. She looked a little hurt, Ellie noticed – and surprised. "Are you so ashamed of us?"

"Of course not!" Kate cried. "I'm proud, so proud of you, of course I am! But. . ." She shrugged, and traced a pattern on the ground with her good foot. "I want people to think of me as Kate first, not as 'Lim Soo May's daughter' every time. And after what happened at Redlands. . ."

"What happened there?" Lim Soo May asked at once.

"What's Redlands?" Ellie blurted out curiously.

"My old ballet school," Kate replied. "And there, whenever I won a prize, or was praised by my teacher, or was entered for a competition, or did *anything*, people would whisper that it was because I was Lim Soo May's daughter. Like I wasn't good enough on my own!" Her cheeks were turning pink at the memory. "As for when I got my place at The Royal Ballet School. . . Well. They all said that was just because I had famous parents." Her dark eyes flashed angrily. "I never wanted anybody to say that again."

"Oh, sweetheart," Soo May cried, sounding distraught at the news. She threw her arms around Kate and hugged her tightly, tears glistening in her eyes. "You should have said something – I never dreamed this was happening to you."

"They must have been so jealous, those Redlands girls," Ellie said. "Like The Royal Ballet School would ever have turned down a dancer as good as YOU, Kate! You totally earned your place here – just like we all did."

Kate turned her mouth up in a little smile. "I know, I know," she said. "It's kind of hard, though, when you feel like you have so much to live up to." She gave her mum a hug back. "Especially as you studied here, too, Mum. I just didn't want anybody comparing us, or judging me for my family, or. . ."

"And none of us will," Lara said firmly, interrupting Kate. "We love you for *you*, Kate."

"Of course we do," Grace said, grabbing Kate's hand.

"Absolutely," Ellie agreed.

"Although, now that we know you have famous parents, we do love you just a little bit more. . ." Naomi said, her lips twitching in amusement, before adding hurriedly, "*Joke!*"

Soo May still had her arms around Kate. "You know, I wasn't going to pick you for the masterclass anyway," she said, "even before I saw those wobbly *pirouettes*. I didn't want anybody accusing *me* of favouritism, so you needn't have worried." She stroked Kate's hair lovingly. "Besides, you can have a private masterclass with me any time you want."

"And we'll have a word with the production editor of the documentary, and ask her not to pick you out in any way during the programme. OK?" Christopher added.

Kate smiled. "OK."

"If you're going to be a star, you'll make it on your own terms," Lim Soo May said firmly. "Am I right?"

Kate leaned into her mum happily, looking more relaxed than Ellie had seen her since Easter break. "You're right, Mum. You're absolutely right."

"It almost seems a shame to go back to normal life," Grace sighed the next day. She blushed when Ellie gave her a quizzical look. "Not that life here is ever dull, but. . . You know what I mean. It feels like all the excitement is over."

"Good," said Kate, with feeling. "Thank goodness for that. The more normal the better! No more fuss about celebrity visitors!"

The girls laughed. They were all in the dorm after their choreography class, getting changed for dinner.

"You know, we couldn't help wondering what was going on, Kate," Ellie confessed. "And we convinced ourselves that you had a secret boyfriend – William Forrest, actually!"

"What?" Kate's eyes almost fell out of her head in shock. "William Forrest? How did you work that out?"

"I told you!" Grace said triumphantly to the other girls. "I did keep telling them they were jumping to conclusions, and that nothing was going on with you and William, Kate."

Naomi had the grace to look rather sheepish. "Well, we kept seeing you talking together and. . . We put two and two together."

"And made twenty-seven!" Kate laughed. "William's sister wants to audition for The Royal Ballet School next year. William was asking for my e-mail address so she could ask a few questions about what it's like here. That's what we were talking about – nothing else." She shook her head in amusement. "Honestly, you lot are crazy!"

"Not such supersleuths, after all," Ellie chuckled, winking at Lara, who blushed.

"Knock, knock!" came a cheerful voice just then, and in came Mrs Hall, carrying an enormous wicker basket. "Special delivery," she said, "for all the girls in Year 7."

"What is it?" cried Naomi, running over at once to have a look.

Mrs Hall opened the lid of the hamper to reveal the most perfect picnic the girls had ever seen inside. There were plates of sandwiches, cucumber and carrot sticks, cherry tomatoes, a bowl of plump red strawberries heaped high, and a delicious-looking dark chocolate cake. "There's enough for you all to have your dinner outside tonight, as a special treat," she told them. "Courtesy of Lim Soo May and Christopher Blackwell!"

Ellie beamed, her mouth watering at the sight of the strawberries. Her favourite! "What were you saying about things being back to normal, Kate?" she joked.

Kate was smiling, too. "Well, I can make an exception for *this*," she said. "In fact, I take back everything I said about celebrity visitors, if this is what they're going to do. . ."

The girls carried the picnic hamper outside on to the lawn between them. The sun was still warm on their bare arms, and it felt to Ellie like the perfect way to end the day as she and Lara spread out the red and white gingham tablecloth on the grass, and Kate handed out plates.

"Oh, Kate," Naomi said suddenly, her mouth full of a strawberry she'd sneaked in while unpacking the picnic goodies. "There's an envelope here with your name on it."

Kate tore open the envelope and pulled out a card with a Degas ballerina print on the front. She read it quickly.

"What does it say?" Naomi asked.

Kate was smiling. "It's from Mum and Chris. It says, 'Dear Kate, we are so sorry if things have been difficult this term due to our visit. The last thing we wanted to do was put you in an awkward position or make you feel uncomfortable. We are both so very proud of you. You mean the world to us and we both promise to be more supportive and understanding in the future.'" Kate paused for breath. " 'We can't wait to see you dance in the summer show at the end of the term — but will come in disguise, if you'd rather we didn't draw any more attention to ourselves!' "

The girls laughed. "That is so sweet," Grace said.

"Wait, it gets even better," Kate told them. "Listen! The next bit says, 'PS Let us know a date when everybody is free and we will organize complimentary tickets for you and all your friends to come and see us in *Romeo and Juliet* at the Royal Opera House'!"

"What?" Ellie echoed, sitting up very straight. "Did I just hear what I think I did?"

Kate nodded, beaming. "So . . . does anybody want to go?"

"Me!"

"You bet!"

"Seriously?!"

"Yes, PLEASE!"

Naomi popped another strawberry into her

mouth, looking enormously satisfied. "Kate, you know I said I loved you a little bit more when I found out you had famous parents?" she asked. "Well, guess what? Now that we're all going to see *Romeo and Juliet*, I love your parents, too! Do you think they'd consider adopting another daughter?!"

Dear Diary,

Everything feels so much more normal now that Kate's secret is out and she's relaxed about people knowing. It's so great to see her laughing again — even though she does keep teasing us about our William Forrest mistake!

I feel like everything's settling down again, thank goodness. I've just got to work things out with Heather now, and everything will be perfect. Here's hoping. . .

Chapter Ten

"Ready, Ellie?"

"Ready as I'll ever be."

Ellie was trying to look cheerful, but inside she was feeling nervous. It was the following Saturday morning, and she and her mum had just got out of their car in the car park of Ham House. She couldn't help looking around for Heather or her exchange group. Ellie had no idea what time Heather would get here, or if she would even find her in the huge stately home and its grounds, but she so hoped she could sort things out with her friend this time. Heather was due to fly out of London to Chicago this evening, so it was their last chance to speak face to face.

Her mum took Ellie's arm comfortingly. "Come on," she said. "I'm sure it'll be fine. I bet Heather wants to make up, just as much as you do."

"Do you think?" Ellie asked doubtfully. She pulled her jacket a little tighter around herself, even though the sun was shining, and sighed. "I hope so, Mum."

The two of them walked out of the car park to Ham House. Ellie's mum whistled. "Will you just look at this place?" she said, sounding awestruck. "Isn't it incredible?"

Despite her mixed feelings about being there – what if Heather really didn't want to see her again? What if this was all a huge mistake? – Ellie couldn't help being impressed by the amazing palatial villa they were approaching. It was a huge red-brick house three stories high, with rows of high windows, surrounded by acres of parkland.

"It says here," Ellie's mum said, fishing out

her guidebook, "that the house was built in 1610. Can you believe it's so old?"

Ellie linked an arm through her mum's. "What else does it say in there?" she asked with interest.

"It was home to the Duchess of Lauderdale, who is believed to haunt the house still," her mum replied, reading aloud. "She had eleven children — eleven! — and was said to be very extravagant and greedy."

"Wow," Ellie said. "Eleven children — that's practically a whole dorm full! What else?"

"Let's see. . . There's a cherry garden, a seventeenth-century orangery," her mum read, "walnut and chestnut trees where a flock of green parakeets roost — wow! We'll have to try to see them. . ."

Ellie had tuned out. She'd heard American accents! As they got nearer the entrance to the stately home she could see a large tour group milling around in the foyer. She tightened her grip on her mum's arm as her eyes searched desperately for Heather ... and then she spotted her, laughing with a couple of other girls by a leaflet stand.

"She's there," Ellie said to her mum in a low voice. Suddenly, she felt panicked and wasn't sure what to do.

Her mum patted her arm reassuringly. "Want me to loiter inconspicuously outside?" she asked. "Tell you what – I'll go and find the tea room. Come and find me in there whenever you're done, OK?"

"Thanks, Mum," Ellie said. "OK. Wish me luck."

"You don't need it, but I'm wishing it anyway," her mum replied. "See you later, honey."

Ellie walked over to the leaflet stand, feeling nervous. "Um ... Heather?" she asked, her throat suddenly feeling dry.

Heather spun around and her eyebrows

shot up into her fringe when she saw Ellie standing there. "Ellie!" she exclaimed, and then she looked confused. "What are you doing here? I thought we ... I wasn't supposed to be meeting you in town, was I?"

"No," Ellie said, aware that a couple of Heather's friends were watching her curiously. "No, we weren't supposed to be meeting up, but I couldn't let you go home without. . ." She swallowed. "Without apologizing. For the day I met you in London. I. . ."

Words suddenly deserted her and she twisted her hands together awkwardly. "It was really dumb of me to bring my ballet school friends along. I just wasn't thinking straight. Afterward, I realized it must have seemed like. . ." She took a deep breath. Heather's eyes were giving nothing away. "Like I didn't care about our friendship. But I do. Oh, Heather, I really do! So I've come to say sorry and I hope I haven't wrecked everything."

Heather said nothing for a moment. "Thank you for saying sorry," she replied. "To be honest, I *was* kind of mad at you that day. Well, not mad, just . . . disappointed, I guess. I'd been so excited about seeing you again and catching up, just the two of us and I felt as if I barely got a chance to talk to you."

"I know, I know," Ellie said, wretchedly. "And I'm really sorry. I didn't realize what I'd done until after I'd seen you in Paris and then I thought it might be too late to straighten everything out – but Mum suggested coming here to try to find you, and. . ."

Heather looked taken aback. "You did that for me?"

"Yes, of course," Ellie said. "I know you're flying home tonight and I just wanted to see you again so that I. . ."

Her next words were lost as Heather hugged her. "I'm so glad you did," she said.

"Thank you." Then she chuckled and pretended to look around the foyer. "Now, I hope you haven't brought Naomi and Lara and all the rest of them this time."

"Lara and Naomi? No," Ellie replied, feeling a rush of relief. "Just me and Mum – and she's loitering inconspicuously in the tea room to give us some space."

"Guys, listen up!" a teacher suddenly called out. "You have one hour to explore the grounds here – and then I want everybody to meet back here for a guided tour of the house. OK?"

"One hour? Cool," Heather said. She grabbed Ellie's hand and called out to her other friends. "Hey, I'll see you back here for the tour," she told them. "I'm just going to have a heart-to-heart with my oldest and very best friend, Ellie. We're going to see how much gossip it's humanly possible to pack into one hour. See you later!"

Ellie grinned as she and Heather started walking out of the house and into the beautiful green gardens. "One hour? Is that all we've got?" she said. "We'd better get going. You first. Tell me everything about the exchange – and I do mean EVERYTHING. . ."

Ellie felt as if she were walking on air as she went to meet her mum in the tea room later on. She and Heather had talked and laughed so much at Ham House, it was just like old times, as if they'd never been apart. And then, when it was time to say goodbye again, they'd hugged each other and promised to stay friends for ever.

"I am so glad we talked things out," Ellie said happily as she and her mum drove back to The Royal Ballet School. "You know, if Heather and I had lost touch, it would have been like letting go of a whole chunk of my life, you know what I mean?"

"I do, sweetie," her mum said, slowing down as she turned the car into Richmond Park, where The Royal Ballet School Lower School was. "Well done, for making everything good again. It takes guts to say you're sorry. You did the right thing."

"Even if I did the wrong thing last time," Ellie said, leaning her head against the car window.

Her mum looked over briefly. "Everybody makes mistakes," she reminded her. "And at least you learned from yours. I'm sure you won't do the same thing again any time soon."

"No," Ellie said, shaking her head. "That's for sure."

Her mum turned the car into the school drive, and put on the brake. "Anyway, it's all worked out," she said, smiling. "Feel better?"

Ellie leaned across to hug her mum. "Yes," she said, feeling happier than she had in a long time. "Thanks, Mum – for everything. For

Paris, and today, and taking everybody to the West End. And *especially* for helping me save my friendship with Heather. Thanks a million."

"You're welcome," her mum said, kissing her on the nose. "I'm just glad you're happy again, honey."

Ellie hadn't been back long before Naomi suddenly came tearing into the dorm, a wild look on her face. "Ms Wells is posting the list for Soo May's masterclass!" she screeched. "Quick – come downstairs, everybody – right now!"

Ellie and the other girls were suddenly in one mad rush to get out of the doorway. Grace had no shoes on, Belle's hair was still dripping wet from her shower, and Bryony had a thick green face mask on, because she'd just decided to treat herself to some pampering! Nobody cared, though. Not when the masterclass list had been put up!

"Oh, hurry back and tell me!" Kate wailed after them. With her bandaged-up ankle, it was going to be a while before she could rush anywhere.

"We'll be two minutes!" Naomi yelled back.

Ellie all but tumbled down the steps to the Year 7 bulletin board. Two minutes? Two seconds, more like, at the rate everybody was running!

"Slow down," Mrs Hall cried in alarm. She was coming up the stairs and leaned back against the banister to let them past. "I don't want any more injuries, girls."

Ellie jumped down the last few steps and ran to the bulletin board. There was Ms Wells, with a big smile on her face, tacking up a printed sheet of paper.

"Who is it? Who's on the list?" Lara cried eagerly.

Ms Wells stepped back. "See for

yourselves," she told them.

Ellie could hardly read the words, she was so excited. She and all the other girls were pressed together in a throng. The paper said:

Lim Soo May's ballet masterclass
Lara McCloud
Isabelle Armand
Ellie Brown

"No way!" Ellie screamed, jumping up and down. She checked the list again, suddenly fearful she'd been having delusions, but there it was, in black and white. She, Belle and Lara had been picked!

"Omigosh!" Lara yelled, grabbing Ellie for an impromptu waltz down the hallway. "We've been picked, Ellie! We've been picked!"

"And me, too!" Belle cried, running up and joining them. "*Oh là là!*"

"Dancing with Lim Soo May – oh! I can't believe it," Ellie cheered, whirling Lara and Belle around even faster. She suddenly caught sight of Grace's disappointed face and felt a little guilty for being so happy.

She broke free from the others and went over. "Sorry, Grace – was that really thoughtless of me?" she asked. "Are you OK?"

Grace nodded. "Of course I am," she said staunchly. "Well done – you deserve it. I'm really pleased for you." She hugged Ellie, then laughed a little self-consciously. "As well as being madly jealous, of course. . ."

Ms Wells had overheard, and patted Grace consolingly on the back. "I know it's hard for those of you who haven't been picked," she said. "Everyone wanted to be chosen – well, everyone except for Kate, of course! – but don't worry. According to the film director, they got such great footage during the introductions and in the observation class that it is likely that *all* of the Year 7s will be in the documentary in some way – so you're all going to be TV stars!"

"Oh, wow!" Grace cried, her cheeks flushing pink with excitement. "That's wonderful!"

"Yippeee!" Ellie cheered, doing a *pirouette* with happiness. "Come on, girls, let's go back and tell Kate. Then I've got to call my mum . . . and Pheebs . . . and Bethany . . . and Heather! We're going to be on TV!"

Dear Diary,

What an amazing day! First of all, I am so happy that I made up with Heather and we're still friends. It was awesome spending quality time together today. She's probably somewhere across the Atlantic right now but I know now that our friendship is strong enough to keep going, all those miles and miles apart. Friendships are way too important to put at risk — thank goodness I didn't end up losing my oldest one! Mum is such a superhero for helping me figure everything out, and making it possible for Heather and me to talk the whole thing through. I'm going to save up my allowance to get her something extra special as a thank-you present.

And then I get back to school to find out that I've been picked for Lim Soo May's masterclass! I keep expecting to wake up, and it all to have been a dream. I am just sooo excited. I can't wait! And then there'll be the documentary on TV in the autumn — gosh, we'll be in Year 8 then!

Oh — newsflash! Kate has just announced that her mum has booked us all for "Romeo and Juliet" next weekend — and she went and got us the best seats in the house!!!! Excuse me while I pass out with too much excitement...!

You know, life at The Royal Ballet School

just gets better and better. I know for sure now that I am definitely the luckiest girl alive!